Born in Asturias in 1963, **Rafael Reig** studied Philosophy, Humanities in Madrid and later in New York, where he wrote his PhD thesis on nineteenth-century literary depictions of the prostitute. Today Reig combines university teaching with his manifold writing and editing activities. *Blood on the Saddle* is also published by Serpent's Tail.

Praise for *Blood on the Sad*

'An exuberant mix of comed
dollop of surrealism' *The Ti*

'A refreshingly unconventional little book which takes the crime novel into a new dimension… a gloriously absurd spoof, amusing, provocative and occasionally touching' *Sunday Telegraph*

'Eccentric, dizzying and wonderful' *Observer*

'Reig's prose threa
writing fizzes with
absurdist dialogue
that follows none
is superb, wisely r
might have draine

P O 4

A Pretty Face

Rafael Reig

Translated by Paul Hammond

A complete catalogue record for this book can be
obtained from the British Library on request

First published in Spanish in 2004 as *Guapa de cara*
by Ediciones Lengua de Trapo, Madrid

First published in 2007 by Serpent's Tail,
an imprint of Profile Books Ltd
3A Exmouth House
Pine Street
London EC1R 0JH
website: www.serpentstail.com

Designed and typeset at Neuadd Bwll, Llanwrtyd Wells

Printed and bound in Italy by Legoprint S.p.A., Lavis, Trento

10 9 8 7 6 5 4 3 2 1

For Anusca and Ana.
For the QSQs, always.
For Chavi Azpeitia,
Edu Becerra
and the chronic friends.

He had decided to live forever or die in the attempt.

Joseph Heller, *Catch-22*

I T ALL ENDED ONE THURSDAY MORNING, 18 November 1999, without the century coming to an end and five days before my birthday. I'd have been thirty-six.

It was almost twelve and I'd made a date at twelve on the dot to pick my mother up and go with her to the doc's. I'd been X amount of time trying to get out of the house. At the last minute I always remembered something: my keys, my purse, the light on in the toilet. It made no difference, I knew: I'd be in the lift, at moment X plus one, when I'd realise I'd forgotten the most important thing of all.

Or what I'd forgotten would turn into the most important thing of all.

My life was like that.

I was pondering these things, with my coat on, the door open and going back in for my chequebook, when I heard the sound of footsteps.

It was two men, one in jeans and anorak, and another in a grey diplomatic-stripe suit but without a tie, belt or laces in his shoes, like a convict.

They were going into the house.

My house, I mean.

The one in the anorak had a gun in his hand.

—The papers, the one in the suit demanded.

Do you wanna know what I did? I did the only thing I could, I gave him them on the spot, of course. Just for the record, I wasn't thinking so much of saving my life (in short, this life) as of my mother, the poor woman, twinges in her lumbar vertebrae and waiting for me in the waiting room, sitting with her bag on her knees and her overcoat on since nine this morning.

After examining the folder, the one in the suit concluded:

—Mission accomplished.

—What do we do with 'er? asked the one in the anorak.

The other man took a mobile phone from his pocket, punched in a number and asked for instructions.

—Mission accomplished, but there's a hitch: the pillock had already handed over the papers to somebody else, he said.

I felt a greater curiosity to know who might be at the other end of the phone than to know his reply. The one in the suit listened attentively, then said:

—Affirmative.

He hung up and turned to the one in the anorak:

—She knows too much, we gotta get rid of her.

—OK, boss.

So the other one had to be a minion, the one who did the dirty work.

He pressed the barrel of the automatic against my temple and pulled the trigger.

I didn't hear the bang. I felt cold, as if a strand of frost were traversing my forehead and threading its way into my heart.

—On yer way, Brains, the chief ordered.

My first thought was, Now you've done it!

Question: was I maybe to blame for being the innocent victim of a dastardly murder?

Answer: negative.

So why couldn't I avoid blaming myself?

—Now you've done it! This time you've really done it! my telltale psyche went on repeating.

—Gorblimey! piped up a squeaky voice I instantly recognised, despite never having heard it outside my head.

It was the Cyclops Kid, his lazy eye covered with a patch and sticking plaster, his nails bitten to the quick and the right pocket of his trousers torn. He was looking at my corpse stretched out on the ground. One breast was sticking out of the low neckline of my blouse. Through the hole in his pocket the abominable schoolboy was fondling himself as, biting his lip, he looked with his single eye at my lifeless body.

—Let's see your hands, you filthy pig! I shouted.

Benito Viruta, who else, the child of my imagination, the main character in my books, those that awaken so much enthusiasm in 'more demanding little readers'.

—I wasn't doing nothing, I swear, Teach.

—Shut up, you. And put your hands where I can see 'em.

—Yes, Miss.

I closed my eyes, wheezed and looked at myself, laid out on the landing, with my bag across my chest, a breast in the air and my coat undone.

There I was, with my whistle-blowing psyche and sulky lepidoptera flitting around, Benito Viruta picking his nose on the sly and my motionless body stiffening and losing heat.

A good while went by before María Eugenia Pestana, she of 2º 1ª, alias The Pest, found me.

She took the pulse in my neck with two fingers.

The Pest had seen too many movies.

Then she brought a mirror she took from her bag to my mouth. I can't have steamed it up to her satisfaction because she began calling out:

—Nooooo! Oh no! No way do I want to see it! Don't make me see it! I don't want to see it!

My blood on the grey moquette, she must have been referring to.

The Pest had read too much Lorca for her exams.

She went bellowing down the stairs.

Nicolás the caretaker came with a torch, a monkey wrench and a chammy leather (I still don't know why he considered such a rescue kit indispensable), and remained at my side until the authorities arrived, a judge and two policemen. They took photos and cordoned off my flat, but it disappointed me that they didn't draw the outline of my body on the floor with chalk as happens in the movies and like they did when Carlos Viloria died.

Finally, two employees in dark suits appeared and transferred me to the Funeral Services packet boat.

I closed my eyes and counted to twenty, like in the school playground, but with the opposite effect. When I opened them again I was sure of it. I was dead.

The End, I thought. The soundtrack went on getting louder while the credits appeared, with their 'In order of appearance: Mum, Her gynaecologist, Dad, Uncle Frankie', and so on until 'Hired killers, The Pest, Policemen, First funeral employee and Second funeral employee'.

I reconnoitred the deck. I must have been invisible because nobody took the least bit of notice of me.

I touched the helmsman's shoulder. Nothing. I thumped him on the ear with all I had. Useless. I stuck a finger in his eye. Negative. I pinched his nipple. Zilch.

Invisible and, what's more, intangible!

We descended Calle Génova to the bike ferry and then headed north. In the distance I made out the watchtower lights of the marinas of the Compounds: Aravaca, Pozuelo, La Florida – the parapets of the powerful.

To the south, the other side of Puerto Atocha, behind the barbed-wire fence of the First Precinct, I saw the black smoke and the flickering of the flames. The fugitive addicts were burning tyres to keep warm as they waited for the end.

We were sailing along the Castellana Canal towards Ríos Rosas. We left the Eduardo Dato Bridge and the triangular shadow of the Chopeitia Genomics pyramid astern.

Beneath the black water there must be the boughs of the trees and those pavements I trundled along as a youngster, before the oil ran out and they flooded Madrid to make it easier to get around. Since then, the Castellana Canal has divided the city in two, like that decision which splits a life down the middle: on one bank, ignorance; on the other, repentance.

On arriving at the mouth of Ríos Rosas we veered to port and headed for Ciudad Universitaria.

I contemplated my mortal remains on the stretcher in the aft storeroom. It was the first time I'd seen myself from outside and it gave me a feeling a bit like hearing your voice tape-recorded: you just don't recognise yourself.

You have to bear in mind I was disfigured from being shot at close range, plus the less flattering circumstances dying in itself involves, like the involuntary loss of bodily fluids, the relaxing of sphincters, the stiffness, the clothing that comes down, et cetera. Even so, I had to admit it: I was a fatty.

Yes, a fatty. I found it hard to say it for the first time without diminutives.

All my life I'd been the classic likeable little fatty.

Little fatty no, now was the time to recognise it: fatty. Period. Fatty. Full stop.

Pretty, they'd always called me.

'The lass's got a very pretty face,' ever since I was little, a real pain, a torment, a torture like the ones we drew at school in our ring binders.

Now in my head I had a hole as big as a fist through which you could see the encephalic mass, spongy and livid, still quivering, like the sunsets I filch from Machado & Company.

I use them to end chapters with and to arouse those chocolate-boxy thoughts that so impress my unwitting and more demanding little readers.

The contemplation of my brain set my teeth on edge, the way white styrofoam or the stuffing in pillows does.

In the Anatomical Forensic Institute a woman with plaits emptied my handbag on to the table. Kleenexes, a notebook, ballpoints, my reading glasses, diary… Missing, of course, was the chequebook that was to blame for the open door, for my lateness and hence for the dastardly murder I'd ended up being the innocent victim of.

On the radio was an English version of 'On a Misty Windowpane',

the old Los Secretos* song I always remembered in the Spanish of
my childhood.

The paintings don't have colours.
The roses don't seem flowers,
There's no dawn chorus
Nothing's the same, nothing's the same,
Nothing's the same, nothing...

I thought about my underwear. I was wearing some discoloured
knickers with the elastic gone. My mother had spent half her time
warning me to always have my underwear in a perfect state of
inspection because you never knew.

—What if they take you in an emergency to a hospital? she
used to say. A bit embarrassing when they find out you're wearing
dirty knickers, my girl! You never know, María Dolores, you never
know.

When I was very young, I indulged in necrological fantasies
on the bathroom floor, knickers rolled up inside the jeans around
my ankles. Imagining myself dead was the only way of getting
to see myself from outside, as if someone else were involved, a
third person, somebody who wasn't an interested party. I'd died
suddenly, albeit painlessly, if you don't mind. In the forensic light
of the fluorescent tube, I was inspecting the contents of my pockets,
looking at my different cards, the calendar, a phone number
scribbled on a cashpoint receipt, and thinking of myself as if I were

---

*A Spanish folk rock group of the 1980s which emerged as part of *la movida
madrileña*, the Madrid cultural explosion of the early 1980s.

— 7 —

some unknown who'd just died, a woman of whom I knew only what was before my eyes, on the outside.

That was what remained of me.

I used to imagine the reactions of my nearest and dearest, what they'd say, the tears they'd cry, how they'd learn to value me. My funeral turned into a big event, the news appeared in all the papers, even my best friends from school came, Marisol Mateos, Fátima Fernández and Maite Munárriz.

Then I realised I wouldn't be able to see it and in that case it wasn't worth the bother.

I returned from the dead, wiped myself with toilet paper, pulled the chain, hoicked my knickers and jeans up and went back to my room to read.

All the books I read were about me, I was always the only character, the same with *Sinuhé the Egyptian* as with *Thus Spake Zarathustra*.

Time and again I was surprised by the coincidence that both Mika Waltari and Friedrich Nietzsche wrote exactly what I'd thought by myself.

Since then I've grasped that this always happens: we're only capable of recognising in others ideas that have already occurred to us.

—María Dolores Eguíbar Madrazo, pronounced the one in plaits reading my identity card syllable by syllable.

It didn't take her long to discover my civil status (married) and my address (Castelló 13).

I was going to warn her I'd separated from Fernando five years ago and that I no longer lived in that house, but my voice wouldn't work.

Invisible, intangible and, what's more, inaudible. Being murdered was beginning to present a lot of drawbacks or a negative side.

When she opened the diary I felt completely and utterly silly. I'm the sort of person who always obeys without having to. Suffice it to say that like an idiot I fill in the 'Personal Data' pages in diaries. I'd doubted about doing it for another year, but in the end I'd again put that in the event of an accident they should advise Fernando Eguilaz, the man who was no longer my husband.

Fernando, the famous scientist, candidate for the Nobel Prize, was at home and, against all the odds, picked up the phone instead of letting the answer machine kick in.

I felt the urge to smoke, but I couldn't take the packet of Luckies that was on the table. My fingers went right through it. Intangibility was annoying. Would I be able to eat and drink? Would I be able to turn the pages of the newspaper or open a door? Would I walk through walls? Would I need to sleep, to go to the toilet? Would I be reflected in the mirror? Would I have periods?

I interrupted this eternal round of questions and paused to contemplate my state. In short, girls, what prettier pass could I have come to?

Luckily I was invisible to other people, seeing as I was naked. The most remarkable thing was I found myself thin. I didn't look like that supine corpse – instead, I'd finally got to be the way I saw myself inside my head.

I was terrific, finally, having lost almost twenty pounds.

This is one of the more comforting aspects, the positive side, of expiring.

Added to which, sans glasses I was seeing perfectly.

Although, on the other hand, being invisible, intangible, inaudible and all, well, old girl, you tell me, it's much of a muchness being fat or thin, with a pretty face or as ugly as sin.

Distinguished forensic experts, muscular assistants, smiling orderlies, men in white coats or uniforms with stripes at my side without turning their heads.

I went down to the entrance to await the appearance, doubtless spectacular, of Fernando.

Towards Moncloa ashen-coloured clouds were banking. There were, as if let fall in no particular order, cypresses, holm oaks, a rocky place, two or three hills and various slopes to start rolling tyres down.

To my rear, Benito Viruta, pretending to cover his good eye, was looking at me and breathing heavily, as if his face were glued to the windowpane, while muttering:

—Macho, macho, the teach is totally starkers!

That was all I needed, the posthumous company of the child of my imagination, that dirty, villainous lad, always with a hard-on and nothing better to do than bash the bishop through the hole in his pocket.

—Take your glasses off this instant! I ordered.

—Cor, Teach, the brat protested.

I saw my butterfly mind beat its wings and gain height. It left by the window and disappeared among those ragtag grey clouds.

In my insides I felt the knot of a strand of blood coming undone.

—My Dasein! I cried out, as if I'd dropped a Duralex glass on the floor, the sort that always shatter like they were a bomb.

—What's that, Teach?

—The Dasein? Being-in-itself or being-in-me, something like

that, Benito, but let it go, you won't understand – which went for me, too.

—The butterfly? Don't you worry, it has to come back, all you gotta do is wait.

—I told you to take your glasses off. Come on, that's it.

He obeyed.

Without the specs, the only thing he was going to see was shifting shadows and fleeting shapes, like damp stains on the wall or fish in deep water, a blurry shoal on the move.

DEAD, NAKED AND IN THE COMPANY of the malevolent sniveller, I awaited the arrival of Fernando, another of the same.

I looked back over the facts that had led to my murder.

In a way it's pitiful: the one time I get off with someone I go and end up a stiff.

The day of my death, Thursday, I'd woken up at 9.30. The words *mother* and *twinge* were resounding inside my skull.

All about me Madrid began reconstructing itself from ten o'clock onwards.

On Wednesday night the city had behaved like the mercury in a broken thermometer. From Puerta de Moros we saw San Francisco el Grande cast off its moorings and set sail for the horizon, rolling like a merchant ship, its dome inflated with wind and two canons sitting astride the bowsprit. Through one of the arches of the Plaza Mayor there was a direct exit to Santa Ana; small bits of the Calle Almagro were bowling down Cava Alta towards Puerta Cerrada; the swell of the Castellana Canal splashed as high as people's second-floor windows and from the transom of a bar on Espíritu

Santo the countryside near the Alberchina Reservoir in the spring of 1975 was visible.

—Another space/time warp, making five on the trot! exclaimed Eduardo. This city's magical.

For Eduardito Sandoval, the lyric poet, very few things weren't magical. Sex was magical, naturally; late afternoons were magical; there were magical meteorological phenomena, above all sudden downpours, and any chance encounter had perforce to be magical, not to mention magical moments in themselves, almost always after the fifth glass of something.

At that time of the day he was wont to repeat that the windows of the toilets of certain bars gave on to another time and space, they communicated with the past and the outskirts.

It may be that he was right, there: you entered a bar in the centre of Madrid and the minute you went to the toilet you found a little window from which were seen unpaved streets, bits of stony ground, tin cans and non-matching shoes with the soles coming off. That's to say, the countryside, no doubt about it, with its main distinguishing characteristics.

As usual, with the light of day the city gradually got back to rights. The pavements returned to their rightful place, the round plazas to the spot they'd become detached from by night, the waters of the canal subsided and the main avenues began rewinding by themselves, like in a film projected backwards.

I thought if I closed my eyes and counted to twenty, on reopening them Johnson would also have disappeared.

I clenched my fists and my eyelids and made a wish. That the individual in question, the aforesaid Johnson, would disappear and reappear in his own house, in his own bed and with his own wife.

Madrid, that city, could be as magical as Eduardito Sandoval liked, but when I opened my eyes Johnson was still in the same position.

I repeated the operation with less complicated wishes, but I couldn't even get him to appear with pyjamas on.

Then I tried to turn him into something different, to replace him by manageable objects of a reduced size, portable, inoffensive things. I asked for him to be transformed into seven knotted coloured hankies. Alley-oop! Into a French playing card, the ace of spades, for instance. Alley-oop! Into the ever-obliging dove that comes out of the top hat. Alley-oop!

Nothing seemed to work.

And if I tried with another man? OK, but who would I prefer to have naked in my bed instead of Johnson?

Carlos. Carlos Viloria, please. Just one more time.

I tried it with men who were at least alive and close at hand, to make things easy, but it didn't even work with Mario Navalón and Eduardo Sandoval, who were living just around the corner.

Conclusion: when it came to restoring certain solid bodies to their rightful place, neither the winter sun nor that municipal magic Eduardo so firmly believed in sufficed. I'd have to do it by hand, by resorting to the tiresome, but certified, procedures of a lifetime: to wake him up, give him a strong cup of coffee, make it clear there was nothing between us and take my leave with a kiss on the lips. He's loving, yes siree, Johnson's a friend, sure thing, but without opening his mouth even a sixteenth of an inch the wind of heart and habit was not going to slip through that crack and give us both a cold from weekends in those charming hotels, the broken dates and the promises for the future, when he'd have spoken to his wife.

No fear, Johnson, we're not the right age for it any more and on top of that we've known each other for ages.

I convinced myself that the most urgent, decisive and crucial thing was to be dressed when Johnson woke up. I eagerly set myself this modest goal, as if it were the sole objective or horizon of my entire existence.

On tiptoe I took some knickers, a blouse and some socks out of the drawer. I picked my jeans up off the floor.

My mother would give me a ticking-off, that's for sure. She was convinced you had to go to the doctor's neat and well dressed, as if it were a formal ceremony. Not to mention the elastic of my knickers, which had gone, or their colour, which had gradually altered in the wash from red to purplish blue, like one of those twilights in verse that provide so much material for hope and reflection to the littlest among us.

I managed to grab all my clothing without a single link in that chain of powerful snores that was keeping me safe and free from coming apart.

I was some eighteen inches from the bathroom door when at full blast were heard the first bars of a Viennese waltz, 'The Blue Danube', I think.

It was the mobile phone Johnson had left on the bedside table.

The owner of the apparatus sat up double quick as if the waltz had activated a spring concealed in his kidneys.

—Don't make a sound, he barked. Freeze, freeze! No movements! No sounds! No nothing!

I'm beyond hope, because I obeyed automatically.

I was standing there, frozen, gobsmacked and covering myself with the clothes I had in my hands.

Johnson started talking in authentic English.

His wife, thought I, and went red in the face.

Also without wanting to.

He'd spent much of the night talking about the woman he called 'my wife, Carmen'. He always said it that way, pronouncing the name between commas, the same as the examples of apposition Don Balbino gave us in school: 'Juan, the Salamancan toreador, triumphed yesterday in the Monumental de la Ventas Bullring.' I think in El Pespunte he managed to flash an identity-card photo of his wife, comma, Carmen, comma, and some snapshots of two boys with sticking-out ears and an astonished look in their eyes.

Touching, to be sure, but what was I doing in my own house, standing there, naked and freezing, while the bloke gave improbable explanations to his wife, comma, Carmen, comma?

I offered up my sacrifice to deliver their two little ones from those, their family-size, fold-out ear flaps.

—I need your help, Johnson said the instant he hung up.

I didn't even answer. Without further ado, I entered the bathroom, slammed the door and slid the bolt. I left the clothes in the bidet and turned on the shower. While I was cleaning my teeth I considered the possibility of escaping through the window.

I'd have been capable of anything as long as I didn't have to see Johnson again.

It's as well not to forget, though, that I was living in an attic seven floors above the Calle Ruiz pavement, which called for a plan B. For example: to remain for the rest of my life in the bathroom, watching the water run and writing with a finger on the steamed-up mirror:

On a misty windowpane
I wrote your name
without realising it
and my eyes were just like that pane...

While I was humming away Johnson was banging on the door.

—Open up! Open up, please! This is an emergency!

I yielded when he threatened to pee in the kitchen sink. I turned off the shower, took my clothes from the bidet again and I came out with my head held high. Johnson was still naked. And me? Would I manage to get dressed some day, that goal or horizon I'd imagined was so simple and within reach?

As is often said, the bad thing about the horizon is just that: it's always the same distance away, however much you advance towards it.

He didn't close the door and I had to listen to the live outside broadcast of Johnson's emergency, including the final vigorous shakings (I didn't even want to think which surfaces he'd be splashing). Why didn't he use toilet paper to mop himself? Why did he persist in remaining naked? Why did I have to lug my set of clothes all over the place while my mother, all dressed up to go to the doc's, sitting in the waiting room, was squirming under the effect of the relentless twinge?

I summed up these and other doubts in an interrogative synopsis that I pronounced in a loud voice:

—Look, Johnson, old chum, why don't you clear off right now?

—Listen, lady, don't take it out on me, I'm not to blame for anything.

Of course. He wasn't guilty of anything. No way. A child. My little angel. A poor little misunderstood soul.

Right then it didn't attract my attention nor did I give it any importance, but now I remember Johnson spoke next in perfect Spanish, with a certain Chambéri accent, even.

—I'm in grave danger, on red alert. I need your help.

—OK, Johnson, whatever you say, but listen: why don't you start getting dressed?

—That's of no importance right now! He was scandalised, but at least he was kind enough to put his underpants on.

I didn't remember those shiny, red, plastic-looking boxers. Their contemplation begged the question: just how much did I drink last night?

I put my knickers on.

Feeling sorry, and still almost naked, I made him coffee.

Feeling sorry for him, yes, but also for myself in almost equal measure, fair do's.

—I need to hide this. He showed me a black folder he took out of his famous duffel bag. Just for a couple a days. No questions asked.

Johnson had always carried, for almost twenty years, a bag on his shoulder. It was the first time he'd opened it in my presence.

—OK, so leave it here and I'll take care of it later.

—It's my duty to warn you that this is not a game. Your own life may be in danger.

—Sure, sure. OK, Johnson, no probs, hombre. Get outta here right now.

He looked me straight in the eye, put a hand on my shoulder and whispered:

—Thanks. Take care. And behave yourself, Trompita.

I almost upset the cup of coffee (a bad idea when you're clothes-less, I know from experience, girls), and let out a cry:

—So you did remember me, Juan Johnson! You've always remembered.

He put a finger to his lips, whistled that song and blew me a kiss from the palm of his hand.

I opened the folder and took a peek.

There were half a dozen official-looking documents with loads of stamps and florid signatures.

I was going to examine them, but in that instant the vision of my twinge-stricken mother insinuated its way into my brain. I had to get a move on. I put the folder in a drawer and took a shower.

Question: to whom does it occur to go to bed with a guy she meets in a psychiatric clinic?

Answer: only to me.

Conclusion: whatever might happen to me served me right.

I was finally going to get dressed, but a foghorn in the Anatomical Forensics berth interrupted my recapitulation of the facts that led to my murder.

It was a taxi-launch of lateen sail.

—Mind out, Teach! Benito Viruta warned me.

Fernando, my ex, disembarked. He arrived in a high-necked sweater and corduroy jacket, trousers to below the knee and polygonal shoes, drawn freehand. It was an elegant funeral outfit from the most recent Cibeles Fashion Show. The press boys surrounded him and took pictures.

—No comment, no comment, he kept idiotically saying, swatting the air as if keeping off invisible mosquitoes.

His overlarge nose and bulging eyes gave him a distracted air. It seemed he was permanently concentrating on his sublime thoughts, his DNA chains and his genetic codes.

An individual who introduced himself as Álvarez Barthe, the forensic scientist, accompanied him to the morgue, where they showed him that body of mine I no longer recognised as me.

He did, though.

—It's Lola, it's her.

He gave him my particulars and an employee filled out the label I had on my big toe in pen. He spelled out my surname and wrote Maria Dolores without an accent on the i.

Fernando strode away, downcast.

The press boys surrounded him once again.

—We've arrived late, he announced in an unsteady voice, wiping away tears as invisible as those mosquitoes with the back of the hand. I can tell you that we are on the point of synthesising neuroprotein K666. With it, María Dolores would perhaps have been saved. Some day, maybe very soon, we'll manage to conquer death. Now I beg you to respect my pain, I'll make no more comments.

He waved away the journalists with an ostensibly imperious gesture.

Fer, dear, I thought, don't act so high and mighty. This is death and it's unavoidable. I know this for a fact, my father was the first scientist to begin researching the famous neuroprotein. Or don't you remember, Fer?

And he gave up: it was a path with no way forward and no way back. So said my father.

I saw Eduardito, the lyric poet, arrive, pedalling with all his might.

He hugged Fernando.

Eduardo Sandoval was crying for real: one tear after another, like precious stones becoming detached from a necklace, all loose, rolling on the floor, trying to hide beneath the furniture, where we wouldn't be able to reach them with our hands.

Death's not very magical, right, Edu? There's no thread to hold the tears in place. It has no meaning or explanation. There you stay, waiting for the girl sawn in half to appear whole again, but it turns out there's no trick, it was all true, she goes on being divided in two for ever and nobody applauds.

The show cannot go on, the 'The End' always arrives before the ending.

Eduardo's weeping didn't manage to move me.

I understood what was happening, but I didn't get to feel it inside.

That shot in the temple had made an impact in the knot that bound my heart to my head, it'd undone it and now the two went their own way: reason in one direction, emotion in the other, and me in the middle, unable to do anything to bring them back together again.

The strand of blood had come loose, like a ladder in a stocking, making the kind of headway that was beyond repair.

'To sum up, the most characteristic thing about schizos is the parsimony of their feelings. They're folk that have an intellectual, abstract understanding of reality but they're incapable of feeling it,' my father used to repeat. 'Folk who never forget that deep down we're just groups of cells or we're all seventy per cent water.'

A schizophrenic was able to kill his whole family, as had happened not long ago, without feeling the slightest remorse: 'I believe life's like a glass of water. If the glass breaks, the water spills, but it goes on existing, was the explanation of J.R.P., a juvenile schizophrenic, after murdering his mother, father and sister.'

I read it in the paper: he got up at midnight while they were sleeping and hacked them to pieces with a samurai sword.

His little sister suffered from Down's syndrome.

They condemned the juvenile J.R.P. to a punitive lobotomy.

And now I was seeing Eduardito crying over my death, but it was incapable of moving me.

On reflection, maybe it was for the best: how was I going to stand it otherwise?

It gave me the shivers.

—Take it, Teach, put this on.

Benito was handing me a lab coat.

I managed to dress and thought: You've reached your horizon, Lola, you've come back home. You'll not reach forty, dear. You won't see the next century in. Checkmate. Game over. End of story.

—Put your glasses on, I told the boy.

The two lenses came to thirteen dioptres, the frames were plastic and one of the sides had been repaired with adhesive tape and wire.

—You look like a chemist, Teach. Pretty cool.

—So you can see me, then, Benito.

—Yes, he admitted, shamefaced. But I ain't seen nothing, I swear.

—Is that so, Benito? Can't we be seen? Or touch anybody, or move things around? Can't we sleep?

—Sleep, yeah.

—Then bleed?

—Sure, Teach, showing me a little graze on the knee.

I thought so. All animals with blood sleep. Aristotle demonstrated it, even for fish.

—Do you know who I am?

—Don't muck about, Teach. Why do you ask?

—Tell me who I am.

—You're the teach, Teach, he explained, all surprised and tautological. The teacher in Matracas, Doña Silvia.

He was partly right, the lad. To the character of Silvia in my novels I'd given my voice, my pretty face, my bust size and my childhood memories.

I thought of telling him the truth, but he wouldn't have understood: the boy was a dope, as you might expect. At the end of the day, what could my sterile, badly cultivated wit engender but a child as dry, wizened and capricious as Benito Viruta?

—Exactly, I'm Miss Silvia, so now you know, watch your step and do everything I tell you or you stay on till September and you go to the headmaster's.

—I promise, Teach, really I do.

—So, inaudible, intangible and invisible. That's quite an idea, Benito.

—There are some things we can do, Teach. At night.

—Stop all the mystery, Viruta, I know you.

—Be careful what you dream, Miss Silvia. Very careful. I'm serious.

—Yeah, sure. The enemy is within: so shoot us, then!

Benito burst out laughing.

I gave it up as being impossible.

I know the story, my father was a psychiatrist. The threat of our dreams, the darkness that surges forth from fulfilled desires, because desire is an endless chain, each desire fulfilled leads to another one and at the end of the chain lies hidden the only desire we don't wish to look at: the desire for death.

It sounded like those hand-me-down thoughts I was wont to put in my books, along with the purplish twilights and those lightning-blasted trees I transplanted in my computer from *The Thousand Best Poems of All Time.*

MY FATHER WAS A PSYCHIATRIST and on getting back from school I spent many an afternoon in the gardens of the clinic, until they extended it and García Femater retired. Later, Fernando, my husband, the great neuroscientist, began working there, and everything changed: they built the reinforced basement and my father began having bad dreams of a night.

At that time there still weren't bars at the windows and armed guards. It was a three-storey house with a brick wall in the Plaza de Mariano de Cavia, beside one corner of El Retiro, where they put a fountain with ducks that had articulated wings.

Those web-footed creatures must have had a hidden motor because they moved their wings without stopping, day and night, although it might be bucketing it down and even when there were power cuts that left the entire city in darkness.

Like all kids, I repeatedly asked myself the same question: do mad people know they're mad? Do they realise, even if it's only once in a while?

I observed them closely but never got to be sure. At times it seemed like they did. At other times I'd swear they didn't.

Now I think they do. After all, don't I know I'm dead?

The only thing I managed to convince myself of was that they had a lot of fear. It hit you in the eye. They looked to right and left, covered their faces with their hands and hid in wardrobes, under beds or behind open doors.

They tried to protect themselves, built up a set of routines they complied with obsessively and had complicated rituals for carrying out the simplest of actions. That way they must have felt safe and free from danger.

They always moved around at the same speed, unable to accelerate or go slower, each at his or her own rhythm, with no relationship between them or with the outside world. Some went running everywhere, never stopping, persecuted by invisible threats; others shuffled along very slowly, although they might be in a hurry, as if a hand of air held them back by tugging at their clothing. Almost all preserved some worthless object they were never separated from, a lead soldier, a cake of soap, a toothless comb, incomplete and disconcerting things, the remains of some prehistoric dig, biface axes or polished stones, tools whose mysterious function we, the ones who're on the other side, that of reason and of the appearance of writing, were only able to guess at.

To me, most of them seemed very frightened people, incapable of drawing any farther back. Their backs against the wall, they did what little kids do: when they closed their eyes they thought other people didn't see them either.

I also soon realised that mad people do recognise other mad people. Maybe they themselves don't know they're mad, but they do note the difference in others, they distinguish between the sane and the mad. 'Ignore him, that one's nuts,' they'd warn me when one or other of their companions appeared.

In the clinic there were three kinds of inmates. First, there were the chronic ones, who were generally very peaceable and often talkative. Among these, the ones who impressed me most as a little girl were the calculators, capable of doing mathematical operations in their heads with numbers of twenty digits or of instantly coming up with the day of the week corresponding to any date they might be given. 'The thirtieth of August 2013? A Saturday, it'll be,' the one they called Señor Hilario stated forthrightly. I checked it in my perpetual calendar and he'd always got it right. To Don Paquito, I recall, you read a list of fifty words of any kind, in any language, and he repeated them to you in alphabetical order on the spot.

Most of the chronics had been another person in their former life, Supreme Court judges, top-notch academics, post office employees. All had survived their own death, had returned posthumously after the demise of the other individual they'd once been, their own dear departed, someone they remembered in snippets, with fondness but without too much nostalgia, a considerable loss they'd now overcome.

Second, there were the acute ones, with whom I had hardly any contact. There were few of them and they were dangerous, they might get attacks. They used to arrive at the clinic handcuffed, after murdering their families barehanded or with weapons bought in the ironmonger's, bicycle chains, screwdrivers or the legendary pestle. They were transferred right away to a hospital, generally a prison one.

Last, there were the paying patients, the 'tourists', who were the most numerous and who weren't even really mad. It was a question of the rich offspring of Madrilenian high society who had problems with the police and the courts. Prior to the start of proceedings the lawyer and a psychiatrist recommended they be confined for a reasonable time. Then they issued a medical report to win the goodwill of the jury, which as a rule got them an acquittal or a very light sentence. To begin with, most of them appeared because they were homosexual, although right away the drug addicts started arriving en masse, until García Femater retired and sold the clinic to Pérez Ugena, who decided to transform it into a rehabilitation centre for affluent junkies. That was when they reinforced the doors, put armed guards and security cameras in place and constructed the basement they called the Rest Unit.

My father ended up retiring in order to manage to get some sleep, and Fernando took over his position.

According to what my father was in the habit of repeating, each person connects best with a type of patient. His were the schizophrenics, with whom he got along without too many problems, no matter how much they had head and heart disconnected. Fernando, on the other hand, always got on immediately with the hysterics. Ever since I was little it's always been easier for me to have dealings with the psychotics, the paranoiacs above all. I never lied to them, never followed their train of thought: that was my golden rule. Señor Hilario whispered in my ear that the doctors were gradually sucking out his lungs with the phonendoscope and I never replied that he wasn't to worry, that I'd restore them to him by injecting him with a syringe so he'd not have complications. 'That's impossible,' I told him. 'Can't you see you're breathing perfectly, Don Hilario?' If Don Paquito said to me, 'Little one, be very careful, they're sending me harmful rays, they put them in my head and screw them into my brain,' I never reassured him with, 'Don't you worry, I'll ask them to stop doing it, they won't send you any ray again, you'll see,' but replied: 'Don't talk daft, how're they going to send you them? By mail? Where from? Come on, hombre, let's be serious, Don Francisco!'

They're mad but not stupid. The only thing you can't consent to is for them to lose confidence in you, which is what ends up happening when you follow their train of thought (maybe because deep down inside they know only too well how mad they are).

When I was at school, the fact that my father was a psychiatrist and that I knew mad people up close fascinated my friends and made them envious, above all Carlos Viloria and Fernando Eguilaz. They asked me questions, they wanted to know, they needed details.

The truth is I even got tired of it; it was seemingly the most attractive thing about me, the only thing that really interested them.

It embarrassed me almost as much as when they called me a pretty face.

I've always wanted people to love me for myself, not because I was obliging, or because they might need me or because my father was a psychiatrist – that was all I needed.

To love me only for myself, but who am I? What am I?

That's another question. My, oh my, butterfly, restless and fugitive psyche, elusive, unreliable Dasein.

Do you love me? To which came the reply, And do you love me? How much? Would you love me as much if I became blind? Will you go on loving me when I'm old and ugly? And if I were deaf and dumb would you love me then? If I were paralysed and in a wheelchair, would you love me like you do now? If they were to accuse me of a horrible crime I didn't commit and I was condemned to death, would you go on loving me?

Ever since I was a little girl I'd ask these questions, to which all of them would reply, yes.

It was much worse, of course, because then I had to ask myself: Who are you in love with? What is it about me that you love, what remains even though I turn into a different person, a paralytic, a killer or a deaf-mute? Where am I? Where do I fit in? What is there about my own size capable of containing me? Who am I? When am I? At what moment?

In the hinge between to be and not to be, in that pause between two lives, is when I've had the fleeting sensation of actually being. I've lived that way, in the intervals, in the interstices, in the space that remains between the different lives I didn't fit into, between being and not being, between believing and not believing, those two inhuman abysses, that uninhabitable desert region Eduardo Sandoval spoke to me about in school.

With those two, Carlos and Fernando, the clinic thing was as if I were the only one with the reader's ticket of a clandestine library, they were asking me to read everything and to recount it to them later, to report on the incidents in those mysterious books they didn't have access to, to remember every page and every line and to reproduce them word for word.

They saw the clinic as a library in which each person carried a different novel around in his head. Some in instalments, since each week they'd recount an even more difficult episode to me and they always interrupted it at the decisive moment, when the protagonist found himself hanging over the edge of the cliff.

The inmates were like Ray Bradbury's book-people in *Fahrenheit 451*, each of them converted into a living novel, as if their existences had no meaning other than that of preserving the poignant and nonsensical narrative they kept repeating to whoever might wish to hear them.

I met Johnson in that garden, shouldering his own novel. I must have been going on fourteen, in 1977 or so. I don't know if he'd be thirty yet.

In a way, my sense of curiosity to go on reading Johnson's novel and to know how it ended has cost me my life.

—Call me Johnson, he said to everyone, as if he were then going to relate the blind pursuit of a great white whale.

In reality the poor sod had enough to do with keeping himself alive.

Like most of them, he was posthumous, he'd survived the death of another Johnson he hardly remembered. According to what he said, his defunct other had been a financial analyst in an investment bank.

He was the most amiable person in the world, he seemed like an English butler struggling to keep the water on the boil for tea while reality is falling apart all around him: bombs are dropping incessantly, the roof of the house is on fire and the master has long since fled.

He was tall, skinny, with green eyes and ash-coloured hair. I always remember him with a bag, all sorts of bags, but always with a bag on his shoulders.

—This is more important than my life, Trompita, I have to guard it.

—What you got inside it, then, Juan Johnson?

It was our secret password: I called him Juan Johnson because I

could never believe he was foreign and he called me Trompita and
sometimes sang me a kids' ditty:

> *She was wiggling her ears*
> *Calling her mamita*
> *And her mama tells her*
> *Behave yourself, Trompita.*

—You don't want to know, Trompita. It's too dangerous. I can
only tell you that one day, when this gets out, it'll change history.

—What history?

—Future history, Trompita! The rest of our lives.

After that you got nothing more out of him.

A few papers with rubber stamps and illegible signatures, that
was what'd cost me my life.

Question: for whom could my life be less valuable than a handful
of pages?

Answer: I've not the slightest idea.

—They're on their way, they're going to slit you open, Teach,
you gotta hurry. Benito Viruta interrupted my provisional list of
suspects by tugging me along by the sleeve of my lab coat.

Apparently the kid didn't want to miss my autopsy.

How moving is childhood innocence, right, girls?

THEY STRIPPED ME. Into a yellow plastic bag they put my clothes, earrings, glasses and the amber necklace I was wearing. The glasses had the right lens broken. They took the label on which my name was spelt wrong off my big toe. A nurse gazed at the elastic of my knickers and their dubious colour with a gesture of disgust. I seemed to hear my mother:

—What slovenliness, María Dolores, my girl! Remember what I told you: you never know.

They measured and weighed me. Five foot one. A hundred and thirty-two pounds.

There were two men wearing plastic glasses who put two rubber gloves on each hand, one on top of the other. They examined my naked body, measured it and photographed it. With a scalpel they made a Y-shaped incision. The arms of the Y passed below my breasts and the vertical bit skirted around my navel and reached the beginning of my pubic hair. They pulled the upper part, as if they were lifting a bib, and put it on top of my face; then they separated the skin from my ribs. One of the men took an electric saw.

—This is the prosector. Watch now, Teach, the callow youth informed me.

He was enjoying it, the patchless eye was shining and he was eagerly biting his nails to calm his nerves.

—Do you like this, Benito?

—It's ace! Pretty cool, Teach. I come a lot to watch autopsies, with the future in mind. When I grow up I want to be a pathologist.

—A pathologist: I expected nothing less of you. Who invented you, after all!

—Now comes the evisceration. The Rokitansky Method: they take out all the organs en bloc, instead of one by one. You'll see, Teach, you'll see.

He was right, they extracted a set extending from the trachea to the rectum. It resembled a tray with pieces of meat on it like in the display units on the bars of bars: chicken giblets, mesenteries, liver and onions, the *pinchos* Carlos liked so much, the ones he asked for in El Acme.

Afterwards they made an incision from behind, from ear to ear, and separated the skin from the head with a spatula, in order to leave my cranium on view.

Take a good look at my skull, pretty face. Look at it and tell me if I've been a lawyer, tax inspector, a systems analyst. Where's my smile now? Look at my teeth, all chipped from clenching my jaws while sleeping. Look at the dark interior of my smile. Look at my physiognomy as it really is, pretty face, and cry no more over my flayed bones. Heart, don't splash my skeleton with tears and remorse.

Pluvious heart, when will you stop raining?

When will you return me to dust, scatterbrained butterfly, when will you give me sepulchre and silence, ash and oblivion, fog and rest?

The prosector cut a kind of skullcap in the dome of the cranium and lifted it with a chisel so as to be able to detach the brain. Once sectioned through the stem, they put it to float in a dish with formol, held with suture threads to prevent it touching the bottom and going out of shape, as explained to me by the loathsome kid, fruit of my imagination and of the insensate activity of that same floating, walnut-like, encephalic mass. They began cutting slices from my organs, bits from my body, the particulars of a tiny, unfinished life. They weighed my heart and opened it up to peek at its content and to check the light of my veins.

My life fitted into those thirteen and a half ounces. That was it all, the content of my motionless heart, the final meaning of my existence.

When they'd done they sent the specimens to the laboratory, stuffed me with slightly soiled sheets and sewed me up. They washed my body with a hosepipe.

It was already night-time and in the building there remained only a guard who did the football pools and listened to the radio. They kept putting on versions in Anglo of old Los Secretos songs. Now 'The Street of Oblivion' was playing:

Down the street of oblivion
roam your shadow and mine,
each to a sidewalk
'cos of life's ups and downs.
Down the street of oblivion,
where the sun never shines

condemned to a night
as dark as it's cold.

I thought of my heart and my head, separated by a broad stretch of water, each on the opposite pavement of the Castellana Canal, making signs to each other from a distance, without being able to hear above the noise of the current.

—Stay here, Benito. There's something I have to do alone.

—I'll get scared, Teach.

—Don't talk stupid, Beni. Sit there and wait for me. I'll come and get you as soon as I've done. Don't you move.

—Cor!

—You heard me, Viruta. Either you wait for me here or you go straight to the headmaster's office.

You've got to eat something, repeated my father.

—I can't, really I can't, Juan. Don't make me, please.

Their voices resounded in the corridor, as if there were an echo in the space I'd left empty.

I'd legged it from Anatomical Forensics to their house in Calle Viriato. The house of my childhood.

—Shall I warm the meat up a bit? It'll only take a minute in the microwave.

It was still in one piece, the joint of veal planned for after the doctor's. The one I was to have eaten with them, as sad now as my empty shoes lined up in the wardrobe.

There I was at last. As usual, I was arriving late and on top of that, dead.

My father had hung his black jacket on the back of a dining chair. My mother had taken off her shoes and put on some slippers.

—No, really. I can't eat a bite.

—Well, something hot would be good for you.

—Right now I can't. Please don't force me.

In critical situations my father was a firm believer in eating at fixed times. You had to keep control – that was his motto. My mother, on the other hand, interrupted all of her bodily functions, cancelled the lot in order to be able to concentrate and to remain engrossed in her mourning, with no interruptions of any kind, with total dedication.

They were in the kitchen, with the table set for three.

Neither of the two had dared remove my plate yet.

They wouldn't have eaten lunch, wouldn't have eaten dinner, weren't going to want to sleep.

On the dresser in the hall was the yellow plastic bag from Anatomical Forensics that contained my clothes, my earrings and the amber necklace.

When she opened it, my mother was going to discover the discoloured knickers with the elastic gone.

Then she was going to lay into me.

I looked at the black-and-white photo in which I'm wearing the tartan kilt and weeping buckets while my father looks at me with almost transparent eyes. In the background water's to be seen. Why was that girl crying? I could feel the touch of the woollen skirt but I couldn't remember what had made me cry.

I thought she was crying for me. That girl was crying for this woman. The one she was going to become. The one who's now dead.

—At least drink a cup of tea.

—All right, if you insist, a cup of tea!

With disproportionate enthusiasm, my father got up to put some water on to boil.

My mother covered her face with her hands.

Her way of crying, her silent, inconsolable desperation, made the legs of the chair creak against the parquet.

—But what are you doing, Juan? Would you please tell me what you're doing? Behind her back she'd recognised the giveaway sound of the toaster.

—Making a cup of tea.

—How many times do I have to tell you I don't want anything?

My father was moving in slow motion, with very precise movements, paying exaggerated attention to preparing a tray with its embroidered cloth, the teapot and sugar bowl. He spread butter on two pieces of toast and put them on a plate.

—For God's sake, didn't I tell you I don't want anything! protested my mother, eyes like saucers, trembling, with a genuine wish to start crying again.

—You have to eat something, Merche! exploded my father as well.

My mother got up and accelerated out of the kitchen with much rancorous slipper-slapping. Down the corridor she went, blowing her nose in a handkerchief she kept in the sleeve of her jacket.

On his feet, alone, my father contemplated the tray in his hands. He seemed to be waiting for the objects to do something, for a signal proceeding from the toast, signs sent by the porcelain, messages on the part of the teaspoon: the words of things.

I've always heard it said that those who remain suffer more. Ha! I'd like to see the people who say this in my shoes. Poor little me, incolorate, inodorous, insipid, like running water, with my own parents weeping and me not able to do a thing.

Not even hug them.

Suddenly, that strand of blood the bullet in my temple had

untied had rethreaded itself and become knotted, tacking my heart and head together.

Something went click.

Mum returned from the bathroom with that face of hers I knew so well: chin up, lips quivering, eyes throbbing like embers and fist clenched, pressed hard against the thigh, as if she'd come from running an errand and was bringing back the change.

The short kind life gives.

She snatched the tray from Dad and began chewing a piece of toast, on her feet, with the same rage she'd have knifed my killer with.

—Forgive me, Merche. I lost control.

—No, you're right.

—I'm sorry, said Dad, putting his hand on her shoulder.

Mum closed her eyes and threw her head back. She sat in an armchair, although she went on holding the tray resting on her thighs.

Without removing his hand from her shoulder, Dad manoeuvred clumsily around and managed to sit at her side.

They hugged each other uncomfortably, with the tray in between them and in awkward positions, the kind that go with bad dreams and pinched vertebrae.

Both of them were crying in silence.

Me too.

At last.

I opened my lips and caught a tear on my tongue. It tasted of me and reminded me of the sensation of being alive, despite the pain, what does it matter: alive. That's all that counts.

Life, this life, my one unconditional and unrequited love.

I felt my soul being soaked in the sadness of my parents' embrace, like a María biscuit dunked in Colacao.*

I thought that if I were to take it out in order to put it in my mouth, my soul would break in two on the way.

Someone coughed behind me.

—What're you doing here, Viruta? May I ask what you're doing here, then? He'd followed me, he was an impossible brat, that one-eyed schoolboy, a real pain.

—I didn't want to stay on my own, Teach. I was really scared.

I saw the strand of blood come undone once more. I recovered my composure. I wiped away the tears with the sleeve of the lab coat.

—They're my parents, Viruta, it's Mum and Dad. They're my real parents.

—I know, Miss.

—No. This you cannot understand, Benito. You only love yourself.

—That's a lie! The fact is I don't have a mother, Teach.

How was I going to explain his egoism to him, his heart of cork, the suffering he inflicted on Almudena, his adoptive mother? How was I going to make him see that he lived shut in on himself, as if he were in a dark basement with a small window at ground level from which he could see only the shoes of people walking by and hear their threatening footsteps? And why right now, when we were invisible and intangible, when there's no longer any possibility of

---

*A chocolate milk drink for children, rather like Nesquik.

redress but the pain in the heart remains, like a tap that drips all through the night?

—You don't understand anything about anything, you know nothing, you don't know me. Benito was furious.

The boy ran off and shut himself in my former bedroom.

My parents went on sobbing, hugging one another above the tray rocking to and fro on my mother's thighs.

I DON'T KNOW IF HE WAS CRYING. All I saw was a lump that looked like a badly wrapped parcel and trembled with an extremely disagreeable sound, like the sudden raising and lowering of the blinds.

That was Benito Viruta all over. In my own house, after my death (or dastardly murder, rather), with my parents gutted, he had to go on claiming attention, he couldn't resign himself to not being the only character.

A small, malevolent being I'd have slapped across the face with pleasure.

The child of my imagination, to make matters worse, my own dried-up, wizened and whimsical child.

I looked at the bed, the comics, the music box and the firmly closed door of the wardrobe. I've never been able to sleep if a wardrobe door remains open.

I looked at the shelf at the top of the wardrobe.

It always made me angry and ashamed to see what was gradually piling up on the shelf: the nurse's outfit, stamp collection, sewing kit, microscope, box of oil paints and all the other things I'd given up on after imagining I was going to devote a vast amount of time to them, maybe my entire life.

When they gave me the microscope I thought I was going to study the composition of cells during the afternoons, prepare my own tinctures, organise my collection of Petri dishes, and in an instant I saw myself at twenty, studying microbiology in a white coat, like now, pushing my glasses up on to my forehead to peer at bacteria down the microscope, screwing up one eye, convinced I was going to end up inventing vaccines or radiation, like a Madame Curie, or even the famous neuroprotein, like my father and Fernando.

Once I'd mentally lived an entire life devoted to science and the announcement of it had appeared in the paper ('María Dolores Eguíbar. World-famous molecular biologist'), when outwardly only a couple of hours or a couple of weeks had gone by, I went back to the microscope, which was of plastic (a toy, after all, a first communion present) and then I got immediately bored, until finally it ended up on the wardrobe shelf.

And it was that way with everything: the shelf was a necropolis, a common grave in which were buried, crushed up against each other, the mortal remains of Lola Eguíbar, painter; Lola Eguíbar, chess champion; Lola Eguíbar, speleologist… And thusly until Lola Líos, pseudonym of María Dolores Eguíbar, the writer who delighted more demanding little readers.

I'd have liked to have had a more absorbing hobby, of whatever sort, to go every Sunday to train at the skating rink, to reproduce scale models or play club tennis, like Fátima, but it's proved impossible. There's nothing that completely absorbs me. I don't fit into anything. Not into a man. Not even into a single desire.

The desires of my childhood always appeared in pairs.

Like all children my age I wanted to be American, like on the telly, but at the same time thin, because turning into an obese American was no fun at all.

I also felt the two desires all girls have felt at one time or another: I wanted to be a boy and be grown up.

From one day to the next I wanted to turn into a middle-aged man. I felt an inexplicable longing to have a belly, to shave in the morning, to hang my jacket on the back of a dining chair, to hear my wife say, 'Darling, you work too hard,' to talk about football, smoke black tobacco and, above all, be capable of cutting myself off from external reality any time I felt like it, just like that, like someone who disconnects or presses a button, click!, by just proceeding, for example, to read the paper or to do the lotto, whatever, but in that instant, thick-skinned and so masculine way that makes it impossible to say a word to them: can't we women see, perhaps, that his nibs is reading the paper? Does it have to be just when he's busy classifying his collection of miniature bottles of liqueur? Can't we wait an instant, even, until he finishes watching the sports round-up on the news? What a lack of consideration! What a wish to annoy! What a permanent sabotage of his most legitimate interests!

Now I realise that as a girl I was very excited about things that afterwards I found out were within reach of anybody, in fact: having identity cards with your photo and signature in them, knowing the names of streets, travelling by metro.

Or being American, as we've all been for years.

Or being a man, without going any farther.

The problem was my two desires had to be fulfilled at the same time, since I didn't see the slightest attraction in turning into a boy, for instance, without being grown up. And so during break times I'd stay playing at *churro mediamanga mangotero*.* Or worse still, option B: to end up being, overnight, what they call 'a middle-aged woman'. Thanks, but no thanks: either both things or neither. So, let me remain the way I am, dear Mother of God. Better to go on like that, living on sweeties and sugar butties, with the kilt and the plastic bracelet that requires five expectant mothers, four cripples, three baldies, two kids in a pushchair and a woman without a hat to be seen passing by on the street, for then and only then will the wish I've secretly made with my eyes closed be granted, while Marisol, my best friend, was putting it around my wrist.

—Make a wish, Lolita.

A wish? Only one?

I've never had enough with one wish. I don't fit into one wish. I'm like a walnut: it's impossible to open just one with your hand. To break one open you have to press two together. To get to the bottom of my heart I also needed two wishes to be granted, one pressed against the other.

Finally, what I feared most, to wit option B, has come to pass: I grew up without managing to become a boy, which ended up with me turning into a 'middle-aged woman', one of many docile women at a difficult age.

And all this so as to end up murdered in my own home – how unpredictable life is!

---

*A children's game in which one team of five forms an elongated circus-horse figure and a second team of five has to leap on to the horse's back until all are seated thereon. Then the first leaper asks a member of the horse's back – whose eyes perforce gaze at the ground – to guess which of the three options – *churro/ mediamanga/mangotero* – expressed as a hand signal, is the right one.

Freudians of strict obedience like my father claim that nothing important happens in a person's life after the age of six. Absolutely nothing. The same thing occurs time and again, that's all, but in a different setting. The same movie with other actors, like one of those Hollywood remakes of the classics.

Search me. I don't have childhood memories. I'm like one of those automatic answering machines in which incoming messages are recorded on top of the old ones. Each new event has wiped a memory and taken its place.

For all that, the movie plot has always been the same: there's nothing my size. I don't fit into anything, apart from life.

To going on being alive, above all else, contra everyone and contra myself. To live, that's always been my one desire, to adopt the form of the receptacle that contains me.

Benito Viruta had finally nodded off in the bed I slept in as a girl. He'd covered his face with his hands.

I leaned out of the window. A young girl was shivering all alone on the pavement and gazing up at the light behind the net curtains, fascinated in the way moths are. Far away to the south the light of the bonfires in the Precincts glowed red on the horizon. There were symmetrical mounds and skeletal branches, basilicas weighing anchor and the vertical silhouettes of quayside cranes that made as if to stab a sky of basalt, dark, cruel and starless.

Then I heard the boy's voice at my back, like a hand on the other side of the wall:

—It ain't my fault. It wasn't me. I swear it wasn't me, Mother. Where are you, Mother? Mum, look at me. Look at me, Mum, look at me…

I saw his dream extend like a puddle of rainwater around his slumbering body.

Benito's dream was sheer, it had the shape of a mountain chain, the peaks handsawn with a topping of snow. On the slopes there were blocks of granite shifting around the way glaciers do, with tiny movements, all but invisible in themselves yet implacable: when you came to realise it, it was already too late. The boy's teeth were shuddering and coming away from the gums each time he touched them with his tongue. I saw his anguish, which was reddish in colour with black fringes, akin to the astonished pupils of a dead fish. I saw a hand with pointed nails some six inches long caressing Benito's back. At first the boy was grateful for the caress, until he realised the nails were tearing the flesh and sinking into his body like ploughshares. The hand began moving and the nails would open deep furrows and make chunks of his liver and his kidneys pop out, bits of flesh soaked in blood as black as a storm cloud.

And so he cried out in dreams, calling his mother.

—Mum! Mum! Look at me, Mum! he repeated several times until he got his voice to breach the wall of sleep and could hear it sounding from outside and wake up.

He opened his eyes, big with fear. I hugged him.

—It's over now, I whispered. It's over, Benito, it was only a dream. There's nobody behind you, there's nothing. Sleep peacefully, Beni, I'm beside you, I'm with you.

I remained awake at his side throughout the night, seeing his dreams and recalling that photo in which I'm crying at my father's side, with a background of water and a jetty.

On the other side of the wall I heard the sobs of my parents: a deep river that never stopped rolling by and in which I was out of my depth.

THE DAY I WAS BORN IN SARAGOSSA President Kennedy was assassinated in Dallas. Marilyn Monroe had already died, naked and alone, in her house in Los Angeles. She and I were never alive at the same time.

I was born on one of those occasions in which History with a capital H suddenly breaks into personal life with a small l, so that then everybody remembers what they were doing at the moment they heard the news.

In my life there's been another, more important bit of news: the coup on 23 February 1981, when Carlos kissed me on the mouth while the representatives of the sovereign people were kidnapped by a civil guard and the American Army began their invasion of the Iberian peninsula.

That's the way it's been for all those my age, the so-called terminal generation, those who still dream in Spanish and went to school en route. History with a capital H transfixed us: the oil ran out in 1979, cars disappeared, the Communist Party won and, following the February coup, Spain joined the United States and Anglo became the official language.

They've recounted it to me time and again. When I was born my father was dunking a Proustian madeleine in his *café con leche*. A diminutive, laryngectomised individual in a navy-blue suit with stripes on the cuff burst in shouting in a metallic voice.

—Turn on the radio, he ordered the waiter. —They've killed Kennedy. They've done for him with a machine gun!

For my father the murder of John Fitzgerald Kennedy remained permanently associated with my birth, with Hermógenes, the orderly, and with the first version the latter gave of both facts, disfigured by his vocal prosthesis.

—In Dallas, Texas, some hired killers, and then he added: Yours has arrived, Don Juan José, it's a girl. Congratulations!

The door opened again and in came my Uncle Francisco, my mother's only brother, whom everyone called Frankie as requested by the person concerned.

—It's arrived, Jota! Congratulations: she's a princess.

—They've just shot Kennedy. They've done for him.

—Oh my God! wailed Frankie, as if the news personally affected him. My God! Jay Eff Kay! This is the end of an era! What's to become of us now?

The end of an era? What did he mean what would become of them now? Jay Eff Kay?

My father couldn't stand the fact that Francisco pretended to know English, nor that he called him Jota. Nobody had ever called him Juanjo, even: they always called him Juan or Juan José.

My father was born in 1930. He was a boy during the Civil War. At night they went to see the executions, because sometimes a woman facing the firing squad lost her head, lifted her skirts and showed the lot. 'What a photo!' the kids would say, elbowing each other, hidden on the embankment. He saw bombings, he saw lepers and he saw the death of his brother Enrique, who was playing with a loaded gun.

He was a boarder with the Jesuits, studied medicine in Madrid and became a psychiatrist from vocation, although he was grateful, when all is said and done, that he was a clinical specialist. If he'd had to live from a professorship, like so many colleagues, he wasn't sure he'd have been able to stand it: the elbow patches, the darned socks, the third-hand Seat 124, reversing your overcoat... He'd not been born for that! Before the oil ran out we had a 1430, the blue Fourteen-Thirty in which we used to drive to the cottage in Alberchina.

He did doctorate studies in Germany, where he came across the ideas of Nietzsche, which made a deep impression on him, as they did on me when I read his leather-bound complete works without asking permission.

He returned to Madrid much changed. He was intimate with very few people. He relished solitude and grew a walrus moustache like his new idol.

When the adoration lessened, and once clean shaven, he finally managed to be admitted into the orbit of López-Ibor, which was what he'd wished most for in life, his one ambition. Fernández-Buey offered him a position in his own clinic, so my father moved to Saragossa and also opened a private practice at his home on the Plaza de los Santos Mártires.

He never managed to adapt to the city and hated with all his might the uncouth nobility of its inhabitants, the basilica of the Pilar, the Military Academy and even the blessed River Ebro.

Mercedes Madrazo, my mother, came along to his consulting room with a hysterical profile. In the first visual examination my father was able to detect a promising abundance of symptoms, as he stated in the clinical history. My mother was hyperventilating and sublimating, her fingers were slender but with thick ends, the nails were turning blue and her eyes getting bigger owing to lack of oxygen, as if she were awaiting bad news or imminent danger. On shaking hands my father noticed a slight muscular atrophy of the outer side of the palm and became enthusiastic.

My mother told him her background. Her father, my grandfather, the heroic Colonel Madrazo, Mola's friend, had committed suicide in his office in the Academy with his regulation weapon, the Astra 400 he'd used in the Civil War. He pushed the chair back from the table, stood to attention and aimed at his chest. Before reaching his heart the bullet grazed the Laureate Cross of San Fernando he was wearing.

My mother, Mercedes, was twenty and felt limitless rancour towards the father who'd abandoned her without even saying goodbye.

The sessions of analysis resulted in a tangle of successive and heated transferences and counter-transferences. Stretched out on the divan, my mother recounted her dreams in a barely audible voice and with her eyes closed. My father took notes with a fountain pen.

It was a very orthodox Freudian engagement: oral, confabulatory and far-fetched.

After six months they got married and my father finally got a post in Madrid, intern in the García Femater clinic in the Plaza de Mariano de Cavia, opposite those tireless ducks that beat their mechanical wings in the dark.

My mother concentrated on the cooking and the chores. She seemed cured, but at once the delusions of grandeur set in.

She wanted my father to do something definitive.

He appeared to agree:

—One day I'm going to find the secret of life and death, Merche, you'll see.

It was the famous neuroprotein K666.

Then Pérez Ugena and the black basement appeared. My father retired and left his post to Fernando.

—It's not a problem. You have to live. To live for real, you have to know how to lose. You have to die. That's the only secret, all the rest is unimportant. It's all right, he explained to my mother and me, looking at us with those eyes of his, simple and mysterious like lunar rocks.

That was when my mother started getting pains in her back.

—You're somatising, Merche. It's not your vertebrae that hurt you, it's the anxiety.

—Whatever you say, Juan, but it hurts just the same.

She got twinges all the time.

Stiff, with the face of a martyr, she insisted on going on making the beds and on stopping eating.

—What you're doing is somatising everything, my father reprimanded her.

—And what you don't know is what pain is, Juan. If you men had to give birth!

It was the same story all over again. By the mid-sixties my father was already regretting having managed to enter the so-called 'orbit of López-Ibor'. The shoe was on the other foot. López-Ibor was no longer a star – he'd turned into the court asylum keeper, the psychiatrist-in-waiting of developmental Francoism, hanging on the skirts of Opus Dei. In the seventies the real distinction for the enlightened bourgeoisie now fell to figures closer to existential psychoanalysis or to political commitment, a Castilla del Pino, for instance; that is, doctors my father's age but who'd managed to play their cards with more cunning.

It was in the eighties, when he left the clinic, that the genetic researches he'd begun ten years before acquired great importance.

My father's problem was that in the last analysis he always felt ill at ease, caught between two stools. It seemed to be his destiny: he'd turn up in a suit to parties where the other men were dressed more casually, in the inevitable blazer and cravat; when he wore a tweed jacket, everyone else appeared in rigorous evening wear, as if they'd agreed on it behind his back. Among the doctors he was a psycho or, as they say, a pedlar of blankets from Zamora; among the psychologists, on the other hand, he was a psychiatrist: the individual who could write out prescriptions, a 'sweeties man', always under suspicion of applying electroshock treatment to poor misunderstood victims of the society they had the misfortune to live in.

This is my father, the one I remember, a man of melancholic gaze, deliberate movements and eyes like stones wrested from the surface of another planet.

Only on the odd occasion, like some instantaneous reflection in a crystal, have I managed to see in him, through him, that other man my mother fell in love with, the young psychiatrist who'd read Nietzsche and was still capable of planning to do 'something definitive'.

At times I ask myself if I'm able to understand my parents' life.

What was going to become of us? What had already become of us all?

My Uncle Frankie was the first to die, at age twenty-five, in a shipwreck only twenty miles from Puerto Atocha.

Hermógenes, that laryngectomised orderly, had a short, harsh life, like those glasses of Gladiator Cognac he knocked back in one; he suffered from Korsakov's syndrome and lost his memory.

—He couldn't keep control, diagnosed my father, who often used one of his confraternity's favourite expressions: control.

And hugging one another, my parents now have to suffer my death, the victim of a dastardly murder.

WHEN DAY BROKE WE LEFT my parents at home, still awake, with their fluvial weeping, impossible to ford, and that difficult embrace, in an awkward position with a balanced tea tray, and went, Benito and I, to the police station in Rafael Calvo.

Commissioner Torrecilla, who was handling my case, still hadn't arrived, so I placed myself behind the policeman on duty while he read the paper.

The neuroprotein K666 announced by Fernando occupied the headlines in the science news. It wasn't going to defeat death, as my ex had gone so far as to claim, letting himself be borne along by boasting and sublimity. Apparently, an injection was involved that was capable of reconstructing brain tissue and so, applied immediately, it would perhaps have been able to restore life to a person with a bullet in the head, as had been my case, say. Its principal use, however, was going to be in the treatment of degenerative illnesses like Parkinson's, Alzheimer's, Korsakov's, et cetera.

Furthermore, it was claimed that it might end up becoming the only antidote to the mysterious green capsules, the neuropoison the dealers had used since the eighties to punish addicts with ideas of their own.

That same night another two dead addicts had appeared, victims of the green capsules. The bodies were situated in strategic places and displayed the inevitable mutilations so as to serve as a warning.

It was the same old story. Two poor devils who'd tried to move stuff on their own account. They'd found one suspended from a coaxial cable in the KIO Towers. The other was crucified a few yards from a Precinct.

That's how it is: for addicts there's only one way out – to die from an overdose asap. While they're still alive they have only two options. Option A: for the police to localise them at some point and to undergo genetic alteration in the laboratories of Chopeitia Genomics in the heart of the pyramid. And this as long as they don't move stuff, because then it's even worse: the dealers will punish them with green capsules. Or else option B: to cross the wire fence and to go into a Precinct, there to await death inside the chassis of some old car, surrounded by burning tyres and broken windscreens.

According to the paper there was a war in Chechnya or in some other vague place outside the Federation, in Parliament debate was continuing in order to vote for the song of the summer, and Terra had just been launched on the stock exchange with spectacular rises. I was happy for Johnson, who'd invested all his money in the company, as he confided to me on Wednesday night after five whisky and Sprites and before taking off the clothes it then cost him so much to put back on again.

He was going to become a millionaire and he deserved it. He'd suffered a lot.

When I was doing my final exams I once plucked up the courage to ask my father about Johnson.

—Johnson? What Johnson? Who's Johnson? It was very strange for my father not to remember the name of one of his patients.

—The man who always carries a duffel bag, the one who says he's a foreigner.

—Ah, Johnson, that Johnson. Keep away from him, Lola, he can be dangerous.

—Dangerous? He doesn't give me that impression.

—Then that makes him even more dangerous, don't you think, my girl?

I found it hard to believe, but at the beginning of the eighties Johnson's fear became even greater. He looked scared, clutched his bag to his chest, looked out of the corner of his eye, spoke in whispers and always sat with a straight back against the wall.

One day he disappeared from the clinic garden.

—He's in isolation, in the Rest Unit. Nothing serious, he'll get over it, my father informed me.

He reappeared in the garden but it was no longer the same Johnson, at least not the Johnson I knew.

It was at the end of '82, I remember because Spanish had just been banned and they'd wired off the first Precincts, set up in car dumps on the city's southern perimeter.

Johnson had put on thirty pounds or so. He moved very slowly, as if he were in a state of permanent stupor. He hardly spoke. The only thing that remained of him was the bag on his shoulder.

He no longer called me Trompita. He didn't even recognise me, it seemed, so that I had to win his confidence all over again.

—What you got in that bag? I asked him again one day.

—Here? In this bag? Talking to him had become tedious, he repeated the questions before answering.

—Yep, inside there.

—All that's left of me, he uttered with solemnity and sadness.

—And what's that, Johnson?

—I don't know, I've never opened it, but they're things I have to look after.

You couldn't get any more out of him.

At the end of '83 they discharged him. A complete recovery, according to my father, who added:

—He's a new man.

A new man: just like my father after going down to the basement of the clinic.

Commissioner Torrecilla still hadn't come and the policeman on duty had been absorbed in the sports section for almost an hour. *Vicente del Bosque wants a change of mentality because football is about 'attitude and emotion'*, claimed a headline. Rivaldo, 'the slippery striker', was suffering from tendonitis in the abductor. Valencia were going to play Barcelona. The Valencia trainer, someone called Héctor Cúper, was relying on his usual formula: 'Work, silence and luck'. Another headline: *Misfortune dogs Alfonso when he dons a Spanish shirt*. Voracious, insatiable misfortune seemed to be, for someone called Alfonso, a dislocation of the collarbone. Spain and Germany, along with the hosts, Holland and Belgium, were going to be the seeded teams of their groups in the draw for the final phase of Euro 2000, which would be held on 12 December in Brussels. This piece of news was very complicated, with attendant coefficients, probabilities and statistics. The policeman clenched his fists as he tried to decipher it.

He was reading with the same concentration that I immersed myself in Nietzsche with as a girl in order to find in his pages those ideas I'd already thought of by myself.

Exhausted by the effort, the policeman went to the toilet and left the paper open at the culture section. I saw the news of my death and also that of Enrique Urquijo:

Found dead in a doorway Enrique Urquijo, lead singer of Los Secretos
Madrid (Ele) – Enrique Urquijo Prieto, 39, lead singer of the group Los Secretos, one of the emblematic bands of *la movida madrileña*,* was found dead yesterday in the doorway of 23 Calle del Espíritu Santo in Madrid, in the barrio of Malasaña, high-ranking sources of the Madrid police force stated late yesterday afternoon. The body showed no signs of violence, but died of the consumption of drugs, according to police sources. A resident in the building where the songwriter's body was found claimed to have witnessed how a young man and woman tried to revive the musician by giving him heart massage, reports Miguel Tomás Valiente. The couple could not be detained for questioning. The composer of 'Cat's Eyes' was stretched out on his back on the ground. He had his leather jacket under his head as a pillow and his shirt pulled up, with his chest bare.

---

*The Madrid cultural explosion of the early 1980s, the irreverent, sexy tone of which is best summed up by Pedro Almodóvar's early films. The 'Madrid scene' is perhaps the best translation, but 'Swinging Madrid' comes close.

So that was why they'd not stopped playing songs by Los Secretos, the background music of my youth, in Anglo cover versions on the radio.

The news item spoke of the band's tragic history, ever since the death of Canito in 1980, with that concert in Caminos which, according to the reporter, was 'the firing of the starting pistol for *la movida madrileña*'. He also emphasised that the singer was technically a fugitive, like all addicts, and that a search-and-capture order had been issued for the couple, accused of the misdemeanour of failing to report an incident and of deliberately aiding and abetting a federal offender.

La movida madrileña! Twenty years later it sounded archaeological, what with the Castellana flooded, the new life and our generation, the last, transfixed by History.

Paul Bowles had also died in Tangiers.

They relegated me to the corner of a left-hand page and in smaller print.

Mysterious murder of the writer
Dolores Eguíbar, the popular 'Lola Líos'

So it finally transpires I'm a writer. Maybe not so much as Paul Bowles, nor as his wife, Jane; nor even as much as Carlos Viloria, my great love, converted into a classic after the posthumous publication of *Profound Deafness*. Agreed, but a writer all the same.

A writer, how embarrassing, like the main characters of the immense majority of contemporary novels, in which only writers or journalists appear, frequently in the guise of private investigators. The authors bore us with so much fraught hackwork and with telling us 'how one gets to become a writer'. We know it by heart: the years of suffering, the sacrifices, the lack of understanding, the faith in oneself, the solitary effort and all the rest.

I've written things, I admit it, but without any literary ambition, as Fernando forever reproached me with. Books for children what's more.

My obituary was nevertheless in the Culture section:

Madrid (Ele) – The popular writer María Dolores Eguíbar, who wrote her books under the pseudonym of Lola Líos, was found dead yesterday in her studio. Eguíbar, wife of famous scientist Fernando Eguilaz, one of today's most important genetic researchers and a candidate, for the last ten years or so, for the Nobel Prize…

And so on in the same vein.

Even to announce my death it was thought essential to speak of my ex-husband. Only he justified the fact that I was granted so much attention, of course. As Fernando was not prepared to admit we'd separated, my apartment was converted into my 'studio', and me into 'popular', while he, on the other hand, went on being 'famous'.

The article also spoke of Benito Viruta, of the 'sales success among more demanding little readers' and of my 'simple and spontaneous prose, lacking in literary pretension', and ended up recalling what was truly important in my life: that I'd been married to Fernando Eguilaz, the genetic researcher, the man who was on the point of defeating death with his neuroprotein K666.

The truth is I've never managed to understand the success of

Benito Viruta, that repulsive schoolboy, not even among the littlest, however demanding they may be.

Viruta had been born nine years ago when I bought a laptop computer on which I wrote at night without Fernando finding out.

When Fernando refused to have children I got down to writing a simple story featuring an adopted child.

I ended *Cherish Me in Dreams* and felt exhausted, empty, as if I'd just got back from a journey.

It was a cruel, sad tale. Almudena and Miguel had a biological son, Manuel, and decided to adopt a second one, Benito Viruta. Shortly after the adoption the couple split up. So Benito was a boy with lots of complexes who was living with his mother, recently divorced, and his sixteen-year-old brother, Manuel.

I made him adopted so he'd be able to choose. I wanted him to be happy, to have the possibility of dreaming up, of inventing, parents in keeping with his fantasies or his needs (if the two things aren't one and the same).

Benito, who'd arrived in his new family at age eight, had no friends at school, and at home he dedicated himself to making his mother weep by trying to make her feel guilty about the divorce. He often succeeded.

Without warning, his brother Manuel committed suicide. The novel described the absence of an emotional response in Benito over the death of Manuel and the suffering of his mother. He realises what's happening but feels nothing, like the schizophrenics. He thinks only of himself. The boy ends up worse off than when he started, ever more alone, his heart sinking, out of reach beneath tons of water.

The story is told in the first person by Benito himself, who justifies all his actions and tries to gain the reader's sympathy, although I rely on the fact that the latter can't help noticing his cruelty and his egoism.

The novel ends with Benito's suicide attempt. Pure theatre. He does it to attract attention, by imitating his brother, and to hurt his mother even more.

Question: what could the littlest learn from Benito?

Answer: nothing good.

Benito, forever full of bitterness, forever thinking the whole world was against him, forever suspecting the worst of intentions from the rest of humanity.

I'd often imagined his existence as living in a dark basement with a single transom that gave on to the street, at the ankle height of people walking by. A cold, badly ventilated room with great patches of damp on the walls; a place where you have to perch on a chair to glimpse the pavement through the little barred window. How would the outside world be seen from there? How was Benito going to be able to love someone? Confined in his blockheadedness, as in that basement where the light of day doesn't enter, incapable of loving, only with great difficulty would he glimpse a mutilated, muted panorama, threatening and sordid, devoid of meaning and therefore replete with evil intentions. How could you live that way, with no purview other than that of shoes resounding on the pavement, faceless footsteps that draw near or move away? How was Benito not going to imagine, atop those shoes, terrifying, perverse, merciless faces? How could you not assume the worst when looking at the street from inside there? How could you not attribute hidden and harmful intentions to all those who pass by?

At bottom, the most natural thing was what Benito did: to duck down lower every day, to protect himself by covering his face with his hands, to hide in a corner so as to parry the blow he wasn't even able to see coming.

And in the meantime, of course, to do the most damage possible, to launch his preventative attack, like those of the Federation.

I let Fernando read it.

—It has a certain charm, he conceded. The plot's OK. Thickly laid on, but OK. A good sequence of events. There's one thing I don't understand. If you really want to write, you have to do so with a lot more ambition, Lola.

—To me it's all the same, Fernando.

—I don't understand, then. I, of course, don't consider my profession a mere pastime, I can assure you of that.

Fernando couldn't understand it.

For him, lasting fame, namely the Nobel Prize, was the most important thing in life.

I didn't think anybody would read *Cherish Me in Dreams*, but I mentioned it to Marisol Mateos and she convinced me to let her. Surprise: she insisted on publishing it, under the charming pseudonym of Lola Líos. And more difficult still, in 'The Locomotive' collection, aimed at youngsters between twelve and sixteen.

More surprises: Benito Viruta, that monster, that pathological case who wanted to be a pathologist when he grew up, delighted the littlest, those more demanding readers, who snapped up the first edition in three weeks.

I didn't get down to writing 'seriously', as Fernando demanded of me. I decided to continue with more of the same: *You're Crazy for Reading This*.

—What I'll never understand is your lack of ambition. What

would I say your problem is? That you limit yourself, my dear, you don't ask enough of yourself because it's not a matter of life or death for you, was Fernando's diagnosis.

Here, he paused for a moment before continuing to speak. He always did the same, other people were only useful to him for picking up speed before launching himself into his favourite theme: himself, his future Nobel Prize, his immortality.

I stopped listening. At the time I was doing so ever more frequently.

You're Crazy for Reading This also became a hit among the youngest.

I didn't go back to writing. I left it for the same reason I'd begun: because I felt like it. Is there anything wrong with that?

That's the advantage of writing instead of being a writer: you write only when you want to.

I thought I'd finished for ever with Benito Viruta, whom I'd stubbornly managed to have celebrate his fourteenth birthday, but on separating from Fernando I sat down once more in front of the computer.

The result was in my table drawer, under the provisional title of *All the More Reason*, three hundred and sixty pages nobody would read. An all-but-finished manuscript – only the final paragraph was missing, the one in which Benito rejects the kiss of Esther Martínez, the ugliest girl in his class, she who was missing the little finger of her left hand, and thereby closes that small loophole through which he saw the world, remaining completely in the dark, alone, incapable of loving anybody but, of course, with every reason: with all the more reason.

Now it's a question of time: once I'm dead the manuscript will soon arrive in Fernando's hands.

How long will it take for him to realise it's about us? Will he hurriedly rewind and finally see what he's always had before him? Will he understand that my novels have, in point of fact, always been about us?

And what are we all about, Fernando, my dear, tell me.

Maybe they're right in the papers and men are the true protagonists in our lives. Maybe we women appear only on account of the script, in order to reply to them or to bring essential objects onstage. We're that way, that's our true Dasein, monthly and bloody. Bit-part players who intervene only to push on the main action, that of the men. We say our lines and then we die or disappear, always long before the movie ends, without anyone missing us. That's me: Lola Eguíbar, Carlos Viloria's girlfriend, she who was Fernando Eguilaz's wife, the daughter of Dr Eguíbar.

I transformed the harm Fernando did me into the suffering Benito Viruta imposed on his mother. That egoistical child, incapable of looking beyond himself, save from that basement he'd shut himself off in, insensitive to other people's pain, was none other than Fernando seen from close to. Benito's mother, Almudena, the woman in a corner, was my spitting image. And the dead older brother could only be Carlos Viloria, the true one, he who was indeed of the same blood, the indispensable martyr.

I ALWAYS THOUGHT THAT on dying my life would flash before me like in one of those film trailers with bits of the main scenes and music that explains the meaning of the images.

No way. There's no soundtrack. No close-ups. No plot line.

Life, my life, arrives thus far as if it'd had to pass through a very fine sieve that lets only the most frivolous memories through, the insignificant ones, those that aren't worthwhile.

The bigger memories, the important things, the decisive moments, remain inside the sieve.

If I think about that black-and-white photo, the one on top of the dresser, in which I'm with my father and I'm sobbing my heart out, it's easier to remember the colour of the kilt I had on than the reason I'm crying. Why was I crying? I've no idea, I can't remember, but that tartan kilt I've not forgotten.

The most banal, least singular things last longer than feelings, states of mind, deep convictions. Or so it seems, at least from where I'm standing, dead, in a lab coat and without being able to touch anything with my hands, except an invented kid, one-eyed and embittered.

Once the wheat of my life is sifted, the big occasions remain on the other side, only the fine flour of the unimportant reaches me. The colour of the kilt in the black-and-white photo, but not the reason for my tears. The song I was humming in my head after sleeping with Carlos Viloria (it was 'With You at My Side I Feel Better', by Los Secretos), but not the words we must have uttered in a solemn voice. (Words of love, perhaps? Verbs conjugated in the first-person plural? Conditional clauses?) The sound of the banging door as I left my home and my marriage, but not the reason for that final row with Fernando.

It's another version of my life, the B-side, consisting only of trivialities, trifles, riddles, alluvial material and silt. Another warp and woof of my existence, woven with minute, delicate threads, elaborated beneath the tapestry on which great events are depicted, those big scenes with soundtrack incorporated.

Of the important things, I remember only, in fact, the words I've remembered them by. I remember memories, things I've already remembered before at some time or other.

Carlos Viloria told me that Marcel Proust was saying something similar with his famous madeleine. That a memory is possible only thanks to what we forget. What we remember changes as we do, we go on changing it every time we remember it, and that's why it'll never go back to being what and how it was: we've lost it for ever by remembering it. The only true memory, the one that remains as it was, is the one we've forgotten, the one that can still suddenly appear, salvaged by a sensation (like the flavour of that madeleine my father dunked into his *café con leche*). We can only disinter intact what we'd forgotten, because it's the only thing that's remained safe and sound, confided to a protective oblivion as in a national library or in a museum, preserved in a drop of dark resin, in the amber of the necklace I was wearing the day of my death.

While I was waiting for the arrival of Commissioner Torrecilla, the man in charge of my case, I couldn't help asking myself the same question over and again: will I now recover my childhood the way it was, seeing as I've forgotten it, totally wiped it like a message on the answer machine?

AT SANTA CLARA SCHOOL childhood is everlasting, time passes artificially, goes forward and back, moved frame by frame with a Cine Exín* crank. It was a detached house in El Viso, a mixed school, we girls wore tartan kilts and the boys V-necked pullovers. At break times the boys play Rescue, war (you have to count to twenty when the bullet hits you, then you come back to life), football and goal by dribbling or goal by crossing. The girls, almost always at *la goma*† or at skipping in the little playground, where the basketball nets are. My best friends were Marisol Mateos, who had retractile thumbs and knew how to spit out the husks of sunflower seeds, and Fátima Fernández, whose tits never grew until almost the end of secondary school. Also Maite Munárriz, the blonde all the boys were in love with. I also had boyfriends: Eduardo Sandoval, who had one of the lenses of his glasses covered with adhesive tape. 'That way the other eye works harder,' he said. And Carlos Viloria

---

*A simple plastic film projector for kids produced by the Exín Company of Barcelona.

†A game played with a rubber strip cut from a tyre inner tube or a round of elastic stretched taut by two players at various heights from the ground. The other players have to leap over the taut strip.

and Fernando Eguilaz. He who was the love of my life and he who was my husband. We played at Egyptologists, at drawing Houses of Torture and at writing literary descriptions copied from Azorín

At break times we held Nuremberg-type trials with a Madelman.* The sentence was carried out on the gallows of the handrail of the stairs, we hung him with the lace of one of Mario Navalón's shoes. We tied the skirts of the Nancys† at the knees and hung them head down, like Mussolini's mistress. Chapas,‡ marbles and the yo-yo came back every year at around the same time, appearing and disappearing at regular intervals like whooping cough and the desire to live. In class I used to write in a notebook:

María Dolores Eguíbar Madrazo
Viriato 5ª, flat 5Q
Madrid
Spain
Europe
Planet Earth
The Solar System
The Milky Way
The Universe
333

---

*An Action Man-type articulated figurine produced between 1968 and 1983. The first models were Foreign Legionary Madelman, Sailor Madelman and Frogman Madelman.

†Spain's answer to the Barbie doll.

‡Different games are possible using *chapas*, the metal caps from bottles of pop, including a sort of vernacular 'Subbuteo' and a kind of 'tiddlywinks'.

And beyond? What more? There I remained.

In the study hour, from five to six, we drew Houses of Torture in our ring binders.

They were buildings lacking one wall, divided into rectangular rooms. In each of these a different torture was taking place. You didn't have to know how to draw faces because both prisoners and torturers wore a black hood. In pen we drew the most terrible punishments we could imagine.

The most terrifying one won.

Room number one: the prisoner flails about amidst horrible convulsions in a vat of boiling water. In the second room, one of the more classic tortures: the drop of water that hits the exact same spot on the head for twenty-five years. Drip-drip, drip-drip, drip-drip... and so on for twenty-five years until it pierces the skull. Navalón says it bores in like a stalactite. Or is it a stalagmite? If I want to be a writer, the first, most urgent, absolutely crucial thing is to enlarge my vocabulary. I'm going to look in the *Diccionario Aristos*: stalactite, it is. After twenty-five years death ensues amidst horrible convulsions. This was the key to Chineseness (or is it Chinosity?): the patience to accumulate a huge quantity of insignificant units. That's why we Spaniards say 'a job fit for Chinamen' when we mean something long and laborious. One drop of water is inoffensive. Yeah, sure, but – wait twenty-five years and then you'll see! In himself each Chinaman is nothing to write home about but since there were hundreds of millions of them they amounted to the 'Yellow Peril' that was talked about so much on Channel 2. Note the fact, my newscaster friends: if all the Chinese jumped in the air at the same time Planet Earth would change orbit. This is a calculation made by NASA experts at Cape Kennedy in the United States of America, our true fatherland. In Basic General Education all us kids wanted to be American grown-ups. In the end it turns out we're the first generation to have actually managed it… and now what?

The Chinese were communists and therefore capable of agreeing and all jumping in the air at the same time just to annoy. The Great Wall of China is the only human construction visible from outer space. *Nota bene*. The Japanese are something else altogether. They're Nippons, they have an emperor and kamikazes. Kamikaze means 'the storm only the gods can unleash'. They perform hara-kiri. Their minister of justice is called Nikito-Nipongo.* Bus in German is 'Subanestrujenempujenbajen'.† The curtains open. Some bloodstained panties appear with a dagger sticking out. The curtains close. What's the name of the movie? *You're Nickered*! The Japanese are craftier. They go around on tiptoe. They chuckle to themselves. They always kill with a wire through the eardrum, without leaving any trace that's detectable in an autopsy. The forensic expert manages only to ascertain the approximate time of death. He looks for remains of tissue under the nails, signs of a struggle, fibres, hairs, defensive wounds. On a blackboard he analyses the trajectory of the projectiles (then he'll have to send them to Ballistics). It is they that make the dead speak: they always know what the victim's last meal was: a Buccaneer bar, two Tigretón chocolate cream buns, foie gras on bread and twelve fluid ounces of Colacao with milk.

In the third room there's an impaling. Fourth room: a drawing-

---

*'Ni quito ni pongo' or 'I'm not saying one thing or the other'. In other words, an ineffectual minister of justice.

†Literally 'Getongetcrushedpushbackgetoff', which doesn't sound as much like cod German as the Spanish original.

and-quartering. In both cases the prisoners breathe their last amidst horrible convulsions.

Second floor. Here it is at last. The inevitable cage with the rabid rats, hungry after weeks without food. Next room: they rip off a man's fingernails with red-hot pincers. Projected on the prisoner's retina are the selected images of his existence at twenty-four frames a second and somewhat out of focus owing to the horrible convulsions he writhes about in.

While I was drawing the House of Torture my desk-mate, Eduardo, was at the blackboard trying to work out when two trains would meet. Train no. 1, the up train, has left Station A for Station B at 2 p.m. at an average speed of 95 mph; and no. 2, the down train, has left Station B for Station A at 4.45 p.m. at an average speed of 70 mph. If A and B are 348 miles apart, at what point along the line will the two trains meet?

The best Houses of Torture were always the tormented Carlos Viloria's, it has to be said. Yes, but in exchange for what? Was it worth it? How many dioptres did Viloria have in his jet-black pupils? Concealed behind those bottle-bottom glasses were compound, bifocal eyes, like those of *Anableps tetrophthalmus*, the fish that swims with half an eye below the waterline and the other half above. Viloria didn't have human eyes, so why was he going to thank God when he looked at himself in the mirror?

I set myself 'Carlos Viloria's eyes' as a mental exercise. Don Balbino recommended we tried with simple descriptions. 'A house', 'A tree seen by night', 'Dancer spinning on the spot' and 'Nude descending a staircase'.

—Follow the example of Azorín, never depart from his teachings and that way you'll arrive at a mastery of prose.

Azorín, the monster of Monóvar, the description machine, always with a guaranteed minimum of three adjectives per noun, whence his oh-so-characteristic style: neat, pure, concise; a Spanish that was polished, chiselled, carved. The descriptions stuck in my craw. What was I going to put? That Viloria was small, hairy, docile; so soft on the outside you'd say he's all wadding. That he was boneless? That the jet mirrors of his eyes were hard, like two beetles of black crystal. To write, for example, Viloria is star-spangled and his eyes, blue, shiver from afar? The pink blossoms, celestial and golden! Azorín and his firm, clean, quiescent Catholicism!

Azorín annoyed me no end. He made me really want to vomit. To repeat. To retch. To throw up the lot.

A few years later, in secondary school, I suddenly became an atheist after reading Nietzsche on the quiet.

Worse still. Anti-theist, as Eduardo Sandoval used to say:

—I believe God exists, I do, but I'm against him. I'm anti-theist.

—But God has died, Eduardito, Nietzsche says so.

I had a few doubts at the beginning of the university orientation course. I tried to convince myself: '*Mujer*, if you were to believe a little, just a little? Come on, Lola, what's so hard about it?'

It's not right, my inflexible, irritable psyche reminded me.

Either we were believers or we weren't. If I believed, then with all the consequences. Fulfilling all the commandments. And vice versa, if I didn't believe, then with all the consequences, too. Neither rewards nor punishments. I'd have to live on the fringes of the slave morality, like Friedrich Nietzsche, but domiciled at Viriato 52. What a panorama, the Superman born in Saragossa and, what's more, a woman, the *Überfrau* of Chamberí, right in the middle of Calle Viriato!

—There's no need to choose, don't renounce anything, Lola. The only amicable, really *human* thing is vagueness. All the rest is monstrous: that's the uninhabitable desert region, Eduardito the tempter whispered in my ear. You have to live on the tightrope.

To believe, sure, but not that much. Not to believe, right, but depending. To sin, repent, sin again. To live on the knife-edge of doubt, like a high-wire artiste, balanced between two inhuman abysses.

That's the law of least effort. It's not right, my menacing, despotic psyche repeated.

—Because if not, you'll end up like Unamuno, in downright agony and with a tragic sense of life that's never ending, Eduardo warned me.

—Don't start, Edu, please.

Truth to tell, I loathed Unamuno with all my heart. I was a girl of my time, why would I be reading Unamuno? Give me a break! Let's be serious.

Unamuno, that individual.

It gave me the creeps.

Unamuno was a guy who signed and dated his bloody paper birds. I'd seen this when we went with the school to Salamanca. Paper birds signed and dated, there you have it. A somewhat small but very conceited individual who sat at the table with a heater underneath, clutching both testicles and a bundle of papers, prepared to artificially demonstrate the immortality of the soul. By my gonads, I don't plan to die, I don't feel like it!

Always, even in black and white, be it within the confines of a page, Unamuno proceeded as if totally convinced he was still at the café, at one of those frightful literary gatherings, true living universities, as Don Balbino called them!

For the incorrigible Unamuno, as for every literary gatherer, the only important thing was to be right, nothing more. The guy seemed to really believe that if he managed to convince his adversary, then he never was going to die, ever. A question of dialectics, gentlemen, of gradually entangling God, of tricking Him, of bombarding Him with syllogisms, maybe of banging the table at the right moment and reminding Him that he, Unamuno, was rector of Salamanca, dear Lord, High Priest of the Temple of Knowledge. You don't know who you're talking to! You are absolutely right, and the Good Lord would finally have to admit that he wasn't playing dice. You have convinced me, He would recognise in the end: the soul is immortal. Yours, at least, Don Miguel, you who have managed to reason it out. As for the rest of you, wake up! Learn from Señor Unamuno. De Unamuno, my good man, de Unamuno! It's de Unamuno y Jugo, if you don't mind, the charlatan would correct, bursting with pride for a particle. Of course, Señor de Unamuno, of course. Learn from Señor de Unamuno y Jugo, Don Good Lord would advise the other examples of creatureliness or creatureship (as you might say; I'll have to check the *Aristos*) slouching at the round tables of the café, sprawling on the gutta-percha like rustics in their nooks. Learn from Don Miguel, since he is surely never going to die. And why? For the simple reason that he has managed to demonstrate it to me with his dialectics.

Before leaving, Don Good Lord would pay the philosopher's bill at the bar: *café con leche* and half a slice of toast, always the same.

How ingenuous is the Almighty! What an idiot! What a noble brute, as we from Aragón say.

As if Don Good Lord would have forgotten the material the café charlatans are made of. On the outside, of the same stainless steel as a fridge; on the inside, the styrofoam they come packed in. I know them well, they're insatiable, pig-headed, bores, idlers, stubborn as rocks of granite or blocks of marble. You can never admit they're right. Ever. About anything. Not even and above all when they are, because straight away they go and put on a bold front. So, wouldn't Señor de Unamuno now seek the immortality of the body, too? The fellow tried to become eternal with his firmly-laced-up shoes, his fob watch and his private professorship in Greek. Hombre, hombre, Unamuno – sorry, de Unamuno! Don't you think that's sufficient, de Unamuno, my friend? Haven't I conceded you enough already, you creature? I get the impression, Señor de Unamuno, Don paradoxical mistery writer,* that we're taking advantage a bit, don't you think?

Yet Don Miguel goes on arguing pig-headedly, page after page, just as in the café, until Don Good Lord has to leave him, not only with the bar bill paid, but also because he's impossible: listen, amigo, nobody can cope with you because you're paradoxical and president of the Leadworkers Union. Do you know what I'm saying? So there you have it, so do what you bloody well like, Señor de Unamuno.

It turned my stomach.

—Don't mention Unamuno to me, Edu, I beg you.

---

*The Spanish is *nivolista* (not *novelista*) because Unamuno spoke of the novel (*novela*) as being like *niebla* (mist), thus arriving at the neologism *nivola* and *nivolista*. The translator's neologisms are (implicitly) mistery and (explicitly) mistery writer.

—Sorry, old girl. You don't have to be like that!

In '79 the oil ran out and life, the life we led, suddenly changed. After the Communist Party's victory and the failed coup attempt, American troops invaded the Iberian peninsula to vouchsafe the transition to democracy. We finally all got to be Americans. They began the genetic modifications. At that time my father believed the answer to the enigma of life, the victory over death, didn't consist in being right, in convincing a non-existent God, but in researching neuroprotein K666.

He indulged in wishful thinking, until Pérez Ugena and the Rest Unit in the black basement appeared.

—Around here there's no way forward and no way back, I heard him say when the nightmares began. I have to regain control.

When he'd managed to fulfil his desire, to learn the secret, that was when he left it all.

Question: why when someone fulfils their desires do unforeseen and terrible consequences occur?

Answer: because in the very depths of our desires there's only bottomless darkness, that one desire we don't want to look in the face.

Beware of dreams! advised Benito Viruta, the brat dreamed up by me, the onanist Cyclops with the bitten-down fingernails.

One day my father told my mother and me the news. He was going to retire, he was leaving the clinic and the profession.

He became someone else: a new man.

He moved his hands very slowly, as if he were transporting invisible and very heavy objects, but he still went on looking at me with his fluvial, diaphanous eyes with pupils as mysterious as meteorites.

When a pencil falls to the floor sometimes the lead breaks inside. At first it doesn't show, it seems like nothing's happened, but the thing is beyond repair.

This was what happened to my father.

Before all that, before the new life, at my desk in the Basic General Education class at Santa Clara School, when there still was oil and we spoke in Spanish, I went on chewing the cap of my pen, in search of Chinese tortures. Let's see, Lola, just think about it: what would truly hurt the most? Think about it.

The smell in the classroom was thick, acrid, pungent. If I passed my hand beneath the wood of the desk I encountered the raised relief of dried bogeys, pointed like stalactites, stuck one on top of the other by successive BGE generations. Or were they stalagmites? The *Aristos* beckoned once more.

At that very moment there was a palpable air of hatred in the atmosphere of the classroom directed against Carlos Viloria. For pedagogical reasons of uniformity, Don Balbino allowed us to take off our jerseys only all at the same time. Either all of us or none of us. He put it to the vote by a show of hands. Don Balbino consulted us democratically on all those questions that had not the least importance, perhaps as a training for what he must have seen coming, ever since that Dodge Dart flew over Claudio Coello with the Admiral* on board, fresh from communion and in a state of grace.

Almost always it was us girls who refused, because we were at the burgeoning stage, with the exception of Fátima.

---

*Admiral Luis Carrera Blanco, the Spanish prime minister, who was blown up by ETA six months after being nominated by Franco in June 1973.

—Are you all agreed to take off your jerseys? Any votes against?

It was so hot that afternoon it didn't matter to us girls if they saw the burgeoning in our vests. I, who was the fatty, was the one who had the most visible burgeoning. By a long chalk.

For all that, a shaky single hand went up on the back row. It had to be Viloria!

The only thing that worried Viloria was that he was ashamed his braces would be seen, simple as that, we all knew it.

Let's be frank, it was true there'd have been laughter, since wearing braces was considered orthopaedic at the time. The tops in orthopaedics. Weren't a few outbursts of laughter preferable, however, to that palpable and generalised air of hatred, that air of hatred you could cut with a knife, that air of hatred you chomped on in the middle of the last year?

Carlos Viloria ended up becoming Public Enemy Number One of Carlos Viloria!

From the back row Javi Jabrado made an unmistakable sign to Viloria: he passed a finger across his throat. A sentence of death by stoning.

On the blackboard Eduardo went on trying to make two trains travelling in the opposite direction along the same track run into each other. I went back to jotting down in my notebook, as if it were the other train, the down train:

The Universe
The Milky Way
The Solar System
Planet Earth

Europe
Spain
Madrid
Viriato 5∂, flat 5∂
María Dolores Eguíbar Madrazo
888

What was there farther within? That was unknown, too. Just
like what there was beyond the universe. Neither microscope
nor telescope: I had no way of seeing myself either the right
way or the other way round. Would what I was searching for
be between zero and infinity? What was the mileage point at
which the two trains would meet? Would Eduardo solve it on
the blackboard? Would Carlos solve it in his flat on Calle San
Marcos? Would Fernando solve it when he was my husband?
Will I solve it now from here?

The bell for break rang.

In the little playground they cornered Carlos Viloria to stone
him. Two of them held him with his arms in a cross against the
wall so that Jabardo and his cronies could gob in his face. Viloria
was about to burst out crying. He trembled, closed his eyes and the
spitballs splattered against his eyelids, his forehead, slid like tears
down his cheeks towards his lips, towards the mouth his sobbing
made him open.

The Twins and Yáñez moved forward, arms around each other's
shoulders, crooning 'Whooooo wanttttts to plaaaaay the whiiiiip?'
Mario Navalón joined them. In one corner Estanis Pérez Ugena
was building a Mesopotamian ziggurat with Cinzano bottle tops.
The lugubrious Estanis, the one who'd end up years later buying

the clinic: mysterious and silent, he went time and again. His look was so deep it could hardly be seen.

On his face, Carlos Viloria's transparent tears were mixing with the thick saliva of the others.

After break it became known: Viloria had peed his pants while they stoned him. Javi Jabardo spotted it:

—He's pissing himself! he announced with a guffaw.

Was it from fear? From rage? From loneliness?

We never found out.

Javi Jabardo later became an encyclopaedia salesman; once he called at my door with his samples. I think he ended up becoming an addict and managed to take refuge in a Precinct, where he'd await death shivering among junk from the oil era, the things of his own childhood.

I added a room with the coffin with spikes facing inwards. A classic: the Iron Maiden.

I contemplated my work, my House of Torture, determined to feel that dissatisfaction which characterises all true artists. Eight hooded prisoners were flailing about amidst horrible convulsions.

Now I see it clearly, but I've always known it: the eight prisoners were the same person.

When I took their hood offs, there was I, the little fatty with a pretty face. I was them all, I always recognised myself. María Dolores Eguíbar Madrazo, amidst horrible convulsions, cooked over a slow fire in a vat, her brain pierced by the deadly Chinese water torture, impaled, drawn and quartered, devoured by rats, her fingernails ripped out one by one and her body pierced by spikes in the dark interior of the coffin.

It was my suffering drawn by hand in the jotter.

The worst was to come, however.

Beneath the hoods of all the executioners the same face also smiled. I recognised myself once again. It was me too, pretty face, little fatty, being merciless with my own self.

Without pity, I was roasting myself on the fire, aiming the drop of water at my own head, impaling myself, drawing and quartering myself, shutting myself in with rabid rats, ripping out my own nails and closing the cover of the fatal coffin on myself.

I was my own Private Enemy Number One.

Question: why was I doing myself so much harm?

Answer: because someone has to be guilty.

Nietzsche says it:

—I suffer: someone has to take the blame.

—You're someone. You're to blame for yourself.

Conclusion: if God has died, then I'm to blame, just like Viloria versus Viloria.

Esteban's school bus, the 'old jalopy', lurches like a ghost ship, a *bateau ivre* that crosses submerged cities: Madrid in black and white, the seventies. Balconies pass by on which there are butane cylinders, flowerpots with geraniums and Palm Sunday branches. Soundlessly, shop windows, bell-bottomed trousers, platform shoes, layered hairstyles move back, life as a whole on the other side of the little window. We advance, dodging galleon hulks covered in lichen, blooming, like Bimbo bread when it goes bad in its plastic bag. There are forests of seaweed intertwined in canopies and attics, sargassos, lianas, rambling and arborescent ferns. The nebulous plankton blurs the property horizon at the end of Generalísimo, where they're putting up skyscrapers with the future in mind.

Carlos Viloria is sitting in the first seat, alone with the rest of Basic General Education and the rest of his life. He has his forehead glued to the glass of the little escape window, below the hammer for emergencies.

Eduardo Sandoval turns round towards us, his good eye showing through the gap between two seats.

—Viloria's messed himself, he who will become a lyric poet informs us.

—You're the one who's a dirty pig, Marisol replies.

—I swear. From fear. He always messes himself. That's why he wears a lining under his trousers, as if they were pyjamas.

—That's not why, dirty pig. It's because the wool of his trousers prickles him. And what's more it was pee.

—No way, it's *caca*, more like. They've stoned him and he's messed himself. Jabardo swore to me.

On the radio they're dedicating songs. From Stuttgart, in Germany, for Vanessa in Miranda de Ebro from her boyfriend José Miguel, who misses her a lot. The vibrato voice of Nino Bravo is heard. On leaving, a kiss and a flower. Esteban manoeuvres with effort, arms spread wide to take in the enormous circumference of the jalopy's steering wheel. Viloria is steaming up the glass of the window: he has a frozen forehead and shining eyes.

He's crying once again.

Arriving one by one until here, through the sieve, are his tears, still hot, quivering, mixed with the saliva of others.

Right now, while Viloria steams up the glass there, he's already dead here, stretched out on the floor of his house in Calle San Marcos, with the manuscript of his unpublished novel on his chest. He doesn't know it yet, but he's the man who will die before reaching thirty. Viloria's now buried face down, as was made obligatory for suicides by the Federation, face to the earth, while the jalopy crosses jammed streets and his warm tears moisten the escape window and my memory.

Let Unamuno come and start arguing now with his paradoxes about the death of this man! Let Azorín come and see it! Let him describe it! Let him accord it three more or less synonymous adjectives!

The curtains open. A man is born, is not happy, and dies. The curtains close. What's the name of the movie?

SEVEN EYES WERE READING the preliminary report on the so-called 'Eguíbar Case'. Two blue ones belonged to Commissioner Torrecilla; another two, black, were those of Inspector Menéndez; two more, which were myopic, hazel-coloured, were yours truly's and peered over the policeman's shoulder; the seventh belonged to Benito Viruta, who was screwing up the other one in order to concentrate on the reading, as if he were pointing an airgun during target shooting.

I immediately ordered him to put the patch back over his lazy eye, he had to wear it at least two hours a day.

They'd fired a nine-millimetre bullet at me with an automatic weapon, an Astra 22. My head presented an orifice of entry in the left parietal bone and a descending antero-posterior trajectory. The orifice of exit had destroyed the occipital. They'd extracted the projectile from the skirting board of the stair landing. The diameter of the orifice of entry was two inches and there were powder burns, which indicated that the shot had been effected at point-blank range or from not many inches away. The expansive wave had led to the loss of more than thirty per cent of the encephalic mass.

—Fatal, of necessity, Commissioner Torrecilla diagnosed.

—Poor thing, Inspector Carmen Menéndez was moved to say.

The commissioner was greying at the temples and had dark eyes and a half-moon-shaped bullet scar on his right cheek. He was tall and thin, still muscular. He was dressed in dark colours, in a jacket and tie, and wore the kind of lace-up shoes that appear singly, without their partner, in the middle of the countryside with the rubber sole half off.

The inspector was dark haired, with a metallic look in her eyes, thin lips and a tailored suit that didn't manage (and maybe didn't try) to hide the alarming bulk of her breasts.

The forensic report said that death had occurred between 9 a.m. and one in the afternoon.

It was right.

The police report focused, on the other hand, on my home.

What provides more information about a human being, their body or their house? Their furniture or the length of their legs? How they've left the bathroom or the contents of their stomach? The posters in their bedroom or the scars on their arms? Where is there more about we ourselves, in our hands or in the things we decide to touch with them?

I remembered my father's eyes and thought that maybe we are in fact outside of ourselves, in the hearts of those who love us: the only place in the world to which we never have access.

At home there was an unmade bed and two cups of coffee with my fingerprints and those of another unidentified person. There were no signs of violence and the door hadn't been forced, not even the bathroom door, notwithstanding Johnson's emergency.

—We don't know where to begin, Menéndez. Much ado

about nothing. We'll see what the husband tells us and what the neighbours say.

—According to the statistics, the most probable cause of death for a woman between thirty and fifty is always her husband.

—Don't start, Menéndez.

—It's a statistical fact, Commissioner.

The husband? Fernando, my ex-husband, might have caused my death?

I'd always believed that in fact we die like certain characters in a novel: owing to the author's simple lack of imagination. Because nothing better occurs to him than to see us off. I considered that we die through laziness, because nobody has either the time or the energy to get down to thinking of an ending for our tiny lives, so they bump us off through a series of allusions, without it appearing in the main plot and without anyone being any the wiser.

Now, however, I had to consider the possibility that my ex-husband had commissioned my murder from the Boss and Brains.

I was about to consider it when a uniformed officer burst in, yelling:

—I've an artist's impression of the suspect and I've positive identification!

They pounced on a piece of paper on which Johnson's face was seen drawn in charcoal.

—Is it based on the caretaker's description? Torrecilla asked.

—Affirmative, Commissioner. The database has already identified him: Juan Johnson, mental patient. He was interned in the victim's father's clinic. It's the same one the husband, the famous Fernando Eguilaz, is at now. Too many coincidences, right?

—The word 'coincidence' doesn't exist in my dictionary, opined Torrecilla.

—Fernando Eguilaz! exclaimed Inspector Menéndez, open-mouthed and admiring.

Johnson was innocent, that I knew, but he had everything going against him: he'd been with me that night, he'd had breakfast at home and had left fingerprints on every surface (including my body), he had a psychiatric history, and not only knew too much, but his declarations would also be suspicious, whatever he said, both in perfect English and the old Spanish of Chamberí.

—It's only a question of time, now: we'll find him, Inspector Menéndez stated.

—Even before you think, if we're lucky. Something tells me the killer will turn up at the cemetery, Menéndez, they always do. It's in all the manuals: it reassures them to see their victim below ground.

—Correct, Commissioner. The operation's all set.

I T WASN'T HOW I'D IMAGINED it so many times in the bathroom with my pants around my ankles, my knickers rolled up inside and in the necrological light of the fluorescent tube.

In my fantasies the weather was never with you. The sky was wont to be cloudy, an unseasonable wind was blowing; my female friends, their hair mussed, kept their hands on their thighs to hold down their skirts; my male friends, impassive, turned up the collars of their gabardines, and in the end it was always raining, I don't know why, as if to bury someone were to plant a strange seed that would have to be watered with a storm so that in the future it might give of its bitter fruits and carnivorous flowers.

Reality plays with an advantage because it knows that whatever it does it's going to be believed. It counts upon this ace in the sleeve: it's always true, it doesn't need to prove anything, so it can do whatever it feels like, a square sun the colour blue, why not, or birds that blaze in mid-flight, and it will go on being true, we've no option but to believe it, whether we want to or not.

So success, for reality, consists in attaining what might seem a lie, what we might find difficult to believe.

Fantasy plays away from home, it has to achieve the illusion of truth, has to make us believe it's real, at least while it lasts, just as a sonnet by Garcilaso or a painting by Francis Bacon does.

Maybe that's why at my funeral there was a winter sun drawn by hand in the concave sky and there were no fallen leaves or grey puddles, but singing birds and sweet-smelling branches.

Amazing but true, what can you do?

At the entrance to the cemetery we picked up a guide, who preceded us on a funerary Bestegui Hermanos bike, enamelled in black.

—La Almudena occupies an area into which the entire city of Segovia fits, he was explaining to Inspector Menéndez. Here right now there are more than a million bodies beneath our feet. The cemetery was built on these hillocks for ventilation, to avoid noxious smells.

There to one side, in La Elipa, I'd once heard Burning sing, twenty years ago, 'What's A Girl Like You Doing in a Place Like This?' Afterwards Los Secretos played, with Enrique Urquijo, I remember it well.

There were half a dozen women standing around the open grave.

—Look, I remarked to Benito. They're my friends.

These middle-aged women had taken up their position all together in a separate group. I was but one more of them, another unfinished female life, another heart at the mercy of men, the innocent victim of another dastardly murder.

Who knows where they come from, they appear when you least expect it, dragging the years, the disappointments and the littlest one's Jané pram behind them, they don't eat a morsel, almost, and

*Jané is a famous pram, first produced in 1932.

they smoke in silence, the schoolmates, the old friends, the friends for life, the ones who wait for you to ask for coffee without saying a word, and only then do they go and let it all out all at once, without taking their eyes off the corner of the tablecloth: I've had enough, if I stick it it's for the kids, we almost never talk, we hardly ever laugh, he treats me like a bit of the furniture…

Before leaving, they scribble on a paper napkin the telephone number that years ago you knew by heart, the number of their parents' house.

Is it always like this? Do you always have to diminish the other person so as to feel you possess them, just like repeatedly folding a piece of paper in two, each time smaller, until it fits into your pocket?

The last time I'd seen Marisol she told me she couldn't stand it any more, but here she was once more, arriving on her husband's arm, wearing dark glasses and carrying a folding umbrella.

The glasses hid a bruise. She'd been that way for years, like a breaking wave, appearing out of the blue to tell how she couldn't stand it any more, disappearing once again on the arm of her husband, reappearing with dark glasses.

Besides Marisol, there were many others who'd brought along an umbrella, as if they also thought that burials are only credible when it rains on the tears and water bounces off the lid of the coffin, splish, splash: the heartbeat of a motionless animal lying in wait.

Nicolás, the caretaker, hadn't brought the rescue kit he'd not managed to save my life with (torch, chammy leather and monkey wrench). Now he was carrying a wreath on whose ribbon it said 'Your neighbours will not forget you'.

—Nicolás Piñeiro, I come as a representative of the apartment building, he presented himself, with his right hand stretched out and the wreath in the other.

I deduced, therefore, that María Eugenia, The Pest, she of 2º 1ª, must have come as a representative of the owners. She was all bunged up, with glassy eyes, and was blowing her nose on Kleenexes she then rolled into a ball in her fist and tossed into her handbag.

My father gripped the arm of my mother, rigid with back pain and the stupor of my death. The two let themselves be kissed and hugged and when they were addressed they moved their lips, but nothing was heard, as if they were on TV with the sound turned down.

Fernando, in a sepulchral YSL jacket and Gucci funeral shoes, embraced my father without saying anything, his gaze inexpressive.

My ex put on what he must have thought was the right face for the circumstances: it looked like the one you have when you're in the swimming pool and you want to hide the fact you're peeing in the water.

Then he looked to where I was, fixing a pair of pupils as lugubrious as drawing pins on my eyes.

I felt a shiver go up my spine.

I gave him a wave until I realised he didn't see me.

I went on being invisible, inodorous, incolorate and insipid, like water, which adopts the shape of the receptacle holding it.

In my case, just a coffin of alloy covered in fine woods on the outside and satin-lined within.

Estanislao Pérez Ugena appeared with escorts and a look of profound dejection. All the same, on greeting people he flashed his most perfect smile, as if it were a family keepsake, of no material worth, preserved for generations with the sole purpose, perhaps, of being exhibited at moments like these.

In complete contrast to my forensic fantasies, very few people were crying or looked sad. Most seemed half embarrassed or offended, and a bit alarmed, what's more, as if they felt guilty about knowing the victim of a murder, a common offence when all is said and done, however much it might involve an 'innocent victim' and a 'dastardly killing'.

Behind the gravestones with blurry names, on the trunks of the trees and beyond the stone crosses, unexpected bursts of lightning glinted.

It was the flashguns of Torrecilla's police operation.

There were also press people who took snapshots of the pain of my ex-husband, Fernando Eguilaz, candidate for the Nobel Prize, imminent discoverer of neuroprotein K666.

As in the school playground, separated from the girls, in the background the gentlemen withdrew to light one another's cigarettes. Fernando joined the group, ready to receive hugs, condolences, the flames from gold Duponts and words of comfort.

There we were, the remains of the shipwreck of the last generation to know oil, we who still dreamed in Spanish, we who'd gone to school by bus: the sixties generation, the most numerous of our history, that inflamed abscess which deforms the population pyramids.

I'd always imagined that our generation, the baby-boomers of the sixties, was going to remain in brackets: that they were going to leapfrog over us, sandwiched, as we were, between those who ran from the cops and the little ones who were born with Franco dead or on the day following the founding of the US Iberian Federation.

Our lot were not of an age to struggle against Franco. When the dictator died (in his bed, despite so much heroic opposition, with his faeces fertilising the long hair of the future), we were still at school. That night they put *Objective Burma* on the telly. Neither did we arrive in time to play a big part in the democratic transition to full American citizenship.

Too late.

As youngsters we wanted to be like the grown-ups: incorrigible Reds, with jeans and Chirucas,* combating the power of the Establishment with Marxist slogans, or else by means of a haemorrhage of turned-on creativity, in the midst of Swinging Madrid, with tinted glasses, music groups and a pass for El Rockola.†

By the time we got to be the right age, however, the grown-up survivors already had Armani ties, an official car and Christian Dior glasses, and the *movida* swingers were collecting their Oscars in Hollywood or taking part in chat shows on the box. They all spoke in Anglo and saluted the flag with their hand on their heart and a solemn, frozen expression on their face, as if they were controlling the urge to go to the toilet.

The rest, the ones who hadn't changed, were buried, many of them on their fronts, punished with facing the wall for all eternity.

Hang on a minute: what'd happened? How was it possible?

It turns out that the grown-ups were now the Establishment.

---

*Work boots made of canvas, with a vulcanised rubber sole, famous during the 1960s and 1970s, used by students as informal footwear in the city.

†A Madrid discotheque deemed to be the 'temple of *la movida*'.

With the Caesar of El Pardo* dead and following the Iberian Federation's adherence to the United States, a generational change took place and the grown-ups took over the driving seat. They were very young and hence very determined to put the lid on things for decades.

Only the most determined of people our age, their own biggest fans, managed to join them, people like Estanis Pérez Ugena or even my ex-husband, the great scientist Fernando Eguilaz.

It was a few years later before they got down to creating financial scandals, state killings and genetic modification programmes for delinquents.

With that obstacle on the horizon, we 'acceded to the job market', as the sociologists say, when there wasn't work, any work, good or bad.

We've been the first generation for whom attaining the same standard of living as our parents was not a real expectation but a wild, almost laughable ambition.

We grew up in the sixties, when there was still oil. We were happy kids, with our Nancys and Señorita Pepys† make-up cases. They were the years of development plans, the Seat 600 and the miniskirt. In the eighties, on the other hand, we found ourselves with no way forward, caught between industrial and constitutional rationalisation and the armour-plated lid on things the grown-ups made.

The majority had to go on living in their parents' house, like

---

*Francisco Franco. El Pardo, a palace on the outskirts of Madrid, was his country residence.

†A housewifely doll who came with her own toy kitchen.

one more piece of furniture, reading the small ads and coldly, impartially considering the possibility of earning a living by doing knitting at home.

Others began the endless round of successive, short-lived and badly paid jobs or the study of the Santa Constitución* and the Gettysburg Address, indispensable for the trials and tribulations of public exams.

That's why, as the sociologists say, we of the 'terminal generation', the last to know Spanish lingo and oil, turned into a problem, into a multitude of individuals 'without roots, without a steady job, without stable relationships, without children and without property'.

Look, we are who we are. A time bomb. A gigantic drifting iceberg. A glacier that trundles along with slow but irreversible movements towards the dustbin of History.

Eduardito Sandoval once said to me:

—I've been down Viriato.

It was the street of our childhood, where we went as kids after school to buy packets of picture cards at the confectioner's between Alonso Cano and Modesto Lafuente.

—And what's it like?

—Well, a bicycle almost ran me over. Now it runs the opposite way, they've changed its direction. It no longer goes up towards García Morato, now it comes down.

—Nonsense. It's us who go in the opposite direction, Eduardo.

—And García Morato isn't García Morato, either. Now it's Santa Engracia once again. It's very magical, don't you think?

---

*The Spanish constitution.

The funny thing is that with time I'd ended up being glad they'd leapfrogged over us. I learnt the value of not being seen: the art of ellipsis.

That was our hope: we were lacking in collective historical clout, that narcissism which makes our grown-ups as well as our little ones so trying. A generational 'we' does not exist and this is the closest thing to freedom. We've suffered the capital H of History without ever getting to write it. We don't know how to conjugate the first-person plural. We haven't participated in either *la movida* or the transition to the US Iberian Federation. Nothing whatsoever, we're no more than people on a one-to-one basis. Solitary and amusing individuals. Men and women society has no hold over and therefore with a chance of being free, although at the cost of being nobody.

That was our strength and our hope: to live in one's own name, individually, without belonging to collective history.

At the end of the day, that's exactly why we've been, without knowing it, a generation, albeit elliptical, oblique, side-on to reality: a narrow street that turns off from the wide avenues and heads nowhere or maybe heads towards life, towards those outskirts of life where the wind's always blowing and one hears the water lapping.

And with the same slogan as that Héctor Cúper fellow: work, luck and silence.

A few of them lowered me into the grave with ropes.

Before they began shovelling earth on my coffin, my mother tossed in a red flower; my father, that black-and-white photo in which I appear at his side crying.

When they all made off I remained motionless before my gravestone.

MARÍA DOLORES EGUÍBAR MADRAZO
1963–1999

That's all.

In the end, it transpires that this was what I was seeking at school, when I wrote my name and address in an exercise book, when it went from me towards the universe and back again, from inside to outside, the round trip, without ever managing to resolve the mystery, the place the two trains finally meet, the problem Eduardito Sandoval couldn't work out on the board.

This is the answer. It's here: the exact mileage point is marked with this gravestone. Like pirate treasure, what we'd been searching for is always beneath the earth in the end, marked with a cross on the map, inside a coffin of lead and zinc.

—Cor, what a pity, Teach! said Benito.

—Yep, it is a bit, actually.

—'Course it is, there were only two wreaths, it's a pity. A real disgrace, Miss Silvia.

Typical of Benito, the basement dweller, he who could see only feet making off into the distance.

—Be off with you, my lad.

The boy started running, covering his face with a hand as if he were afraid I might hit him.

Then I saw him.

Johnson was arriving in a gabardine and without a bag on his shoulder, which gave him an even more vulnerable look. He seemed like an upside-down tree, he walked with the skeletal branches and his grey hair waved around in the air like a recently unearthed root. He'd slept for various days with his clothes on, that was for sure. In his hand he had a few tiny wild flowers pulled up from ditches or municipal parks.

He deposited them before my grave and whistled that song:

She was wiggling her ears
Calling her mamita
And her mama tells her
Behave yourself, Trompita.

He whistled low, eyes closed and fingers entwined, as if he were praying.

I'd liked to have cried, but the strand of blood remained undone and on top of that I had to run to catch up with Benito and Torrecilla.

All I needed was to get lost in the cemetery I was buried in, without being able to ask anyone, inaudible, invisible, in my white coat and treading barefoot on more than a million bodies (according to the latest statistics) buried in a labyrinth the size of Segovia.

Suddenly I realised: Johnson and I were not alone.

Doors hidden in the trunks of cypresses opened and out stepped ten plainclothes policemen.

Torrecilla's police operation.

They handcuffed Johnson and radioed the commissioner.

A T THE POLICE STATION they spent the afternoon interrogating Johnson.

—I killed her, was the first thing he said, extending his hands palms uppermost, I don't know whether so they'd handcuff him or to show they were stained with my innocent blood.

Then he explained that because he'd left me those papers he felt responsible for my death.

—What papers? asked Torrecilla.

As Johnson began giving explanations the commissioner gradually became less and less interested. So there were some papers that would change History, so there was what remained of the man himself, what remained of his life, so there was the biggest secret we'd ever faced…

They asked him to describe that final night.

—I met Trompita, María Dolores, in El Acme, around two in the morning, it'd be. She was with a friend, a lyric poet, someone called Eduardo. The three of us talked together and in the end she invited me back to her place. In the morning I left very early, but before leaving I killed her, left her the papers. It was me! I'm guilty!

—Case closed, Torrecilla stated categorically. It's obvious we're faced with the typical homicidal psychopath.

Inspector Menéndez offered herself as a volunteer to deliver the news in person to my ex-husband, the famous scientist. As she said it, her eyes were shining.

Johnson they took back to the clinic, shackled hand and foot.

On a wooden bench in the hallway sat his wife, comma, Carmen, comma, accompanied by her two boys with ears of a poignant, almost aeronautical, size.

Dragging our feet, Benito and I returned to my parents' house.

The commissioner had already informed them of Johnson's detention, but my father didn't agree.

—Johnson's incapable of killing somebody, Merche. Incapable. We're going to get to the bottom of this, I assure you, he said to my mother.

—Johnson's mad, Juan.

—Yes, of course, but not that mad, not in that way. Why would Johnson kill Lola? It makes no sense.

—Calm down, Juan. We have to accept it. Now we need to sleep.

They didn't have dinner, although my father insisted on it; each took a sleeping pill, sipping the same glass of water, and they went off to their bedroom.

—We've got to sleep, too, Benito.

—But I'm not sleepy, Teach, he lied.

His eyes were closing but he made a stubborn effort to stay awake, changing position all the time and blinking with ever-growing speed.

—Come on, off to bed with you, my lad. Look, I'm going to lie down for a bit.

—You sleep, Señorita Silvia, I'm not in the least bit sleepy.

—Stretch out, Beni. Close your eyes.

—All right! He did so grudgingly, on my bed when I was a girl.

—Think of a river. Imagine a river. Do you see it? Are you seeing it?

—Sure I see it, said the boy with the closed eyes.

—It's the afternoon, Benito. The sun's very low, the shadows are very long. Do you see your shadow, see where it gets to? Your shadow already touches the shadow of the trees. Your head is the top of a tree. Listen to the water, Benito. Do you hear the river lapping?

He said yes in a thin voice.

—Enter the river. Are you in it? The water's cold, isn't it? Do you see your shadow beneath the water, on the river bed, on the stones? Do you see it? Yes?

The boy hardly moved his head now.

—Now close your eyes, Benito, close your eyes once more, but there, in the water.

He started snoring.

As I was going towards the kitchen I heard the faint voice of Benito behind me. He was talking in his sleep:

—Mum, I see you, there you are, it's my mother. In the Arco Cinegio.* My mother holds the wall in place with her body, my mother, standing, props up the stones and my heart, all night and every night. My heart falls, the wall lurches. She's that one in the corner, that's Mum, she's got two teeth missing, her tears have made the Rimmel run and her skin's very pale. Mum's white as leprosy. If

---

*A still-extant Roman gateway in Saragossa.

you look my way you'll recognise me, Mother. It's me, Mum. Mum, look at me. Look at me. Please, Mum. Mum!

Beneath the eyelids his eyes were moving very fast. He was clenching his fists. He trembled.

—Mum? he asked, gradually waking up.

—Everything's fine, Benito. Sleep. Sleep in peace. It's Miss Silvia, I'm at your side.

I hugged him.

—I'm afraid to go to sleep, Teach.

—It's all right, Beni, It's all right.

Was he doing it on purpose? I couldn't believe it. I was hugging and consoling him and the brat was surreptitiously taking advantage of it to touch my backside. Without knowing?

I decided to give him the benefit of the doubt, tucked him up in the blanket and moved away from the bed.

—So, you and I can touch each other, then? I asked.

—Of course, Teach, just like we see and we hear one another.

He'd gone red. At the time I thought it was for having touched my backside on purpose.

Now I know he was hiding information from me.

He was an impossible kid. He lied without stopping but suffered for real. What was I going to do with him? Make him face the wall in punishment? Bury him face down?

—Come on, now go to sleep, I ordered.

I left the bedroom so as not to see his answerless dreams and his meaningless suffering.

Down the corridor I sensed the density of my sleeping parents' breathing. The parquet creaked. There was a swell at the height of the skirting board. The high tide of their dreams was flooding the hall, inundating the house to above the radiators and splashing me in the face with drops of salty water.

My father was having spiral-shaped dreams that advanced towards the far end of the apartment while, fast asleep, he changed position, turning over in bed as if to screw himself ever deeper into it.

My mother's dreams were brief and obscure, they gushed forth in spurts, like arterial blood, sticking in her throat and making her cough in her sleep.

I saw a man whose head had been ripped off by a shell and who went on walking as if nothing had happened; I saw a woman who lifted her skirts above her waist and was wearing nothing underneath. The naked woman was laughing dementedly until the captain gave the order and the firing squad opened fire. They shot with cameras instead of rifles.

They must have been the childhood memories of my father, during the Civil War.

Next I saw him immobile, with bent head, looking at the closed door with the Rest Unit sign on it. I saw my father's hand opening the door.

Then he called out in his dream, without managing to wake up.

I saw a girl of two or three. She was laughing. She was the most beautiful child I'd ever seen in my life. And she was happy, all you had to do was look at her shining eyes and her smile. She raised her hands and moved the fingers in front of her own face, contemplated them with astonishment, as if they weren't hers or she didn't know what to use them for.

Only when I saw it was my mother who held the girl in her arms did I realise that that girl was me.

It was impossible to recognise me.

Dreamed up by the love of my mother, she seemed like someone else.

Later on the girl had her back to me. She turned her head round very slowly and I saw her face.

Now she frightened me. Her laughter had turned into the demented guffaws of the woman who denuded herself in front of the firing squad and in front of the kids hidden on the embankment. Now she had bloodshot eyes, there were fangs sticking out from between her lips and the skin of her face was covered in scabs, pustules and worms, which were wriggling across her cheeks from side to side.

The monstrous girl was still laughing.

I realised this child was in my mother's dream and in my father's at the same time, she was their intersection, the delta in which their two dreams met before flowing into the one indifferent, shoreless sea.

My mother began coughing. My father was calling out.

Me, I felt like crying, but I couldn't: the knot of the strand of blood remained undone.

I didn't get a wink of sleep.

I spent the night keeping an eye on the interlaced dreams of my parents and the tenacious and solitary dream of the only offspring of my imagination.

In the morning my father got dressed very early. My mother was still in bed when he took his leave of her:

—We're not going to give up, Merche. I know just the person we need.

I T WAS HARD TO BELIEVE anybody would expect help from such a fellow. That he would call this individual 'just the person we need' made me doubt my father's good sense.

The detective was drunk, dishevelled and in crumpled clothes, although it wasn't yet ten in the morning. He was wearing a yellow polyester shirt with the sleeves rolled up, pinstriped trousers and a green tie, knotted in such a way that the wider end had remained very short, while the narrower one extended over his massive belly until reaching his unzipped fly.

He wasn't even wearing a belt.

—Good morning, Mr Clot, my father said in Anglo.

—Dr Eguíbar, it's been a long time! I'm glad to see you again, take a seat. What can I do for you?

Clot didn't even bother to hide a strong Spanish accent.

My father explained my murder to him, the accusation against Johnson and his belief that the real culprit went unpunished and was walking the streets.

Before replying Clot lit a cigarette and shrugged his shoulders.

—And what's it to you, Eguíbar, my old friend? Why do you want to know?

—You've got a daughter, too.

—She's no longer the same. When I came along to your clinic she was suffering from cerebral palsy. Now she lives in Valencia, a long way away from me. She was cured thanks to those green capsules. They're not just used to kill, as you know. She's well, recovered, but she's disappeared from my life, it's as if she were dead.

—I remember it well. At the time I helped you, isn't that right, Charlie?

—I owe you one: enough said.

—Then help me find the killer. I need to know.

—To know! To know! To know! Always the same old refrain. What an obsession. They all want to know, don't ask me why. Listen, Eguíbar, my brother: when knowing increases, pain increases... Do you fancy a drink?

My father shook his head. Clot opened the H–I drawer of the filing cabinet and generously served himself from a bottle of Loch Lomond he had hidden there.

—The letter I of Irremediable, he murmured.

He drank avidly and then he addressed my father in the lingo:

—Before, you were one of those who prefer not to know, amigo Eguíbar, I remember it well. You advised me to take my daughter out of the clinic and then you resigned. You didn't want to know what they were doing with your discoveries: the green capsules. You preferred remaining in the dark, isn't that right? You saved my daughter but you chose to know no more, you didn't want the pain to increase, isn't that true?

—Before, my daughter was alive, Clot. Alive.

The fellow poured himself another glass of whisky and sipped it in silence, his eyes closed, as if he were meditating.

—OK, Doc. I'll help you, he said at last.

They shook hands.

When my father left the office Benito and I stayed behind with Charlie Clot, who went back to consulting the filing cabinet at the same letter.

—Illimitable, he muttered to himself.

It was a very prolonged consultation.

He drank in a rage, totally absorbed and gripping the glass as if he wanted to shatter it in his fist. It seemed as if he were trying to wash away his hopes with whisky, as one might shake a carpet out of the window. Suddenly, from the hallstand he plucked a horrible jacket in a cobalt-blue synthetic material.

His secretary stood in his way.

—Señor Clot, permit me to accompany you. I can be of help.

She was a woman my age, with very small breasts, a tailored suit and stiletto-heeled shoes.

—You win, Miss Koebnick. Just this once. Keep your mouth shut: look and learn.

—I won't let you down, Chief, she said enthusiastically, putting her hand on Clot's arm.

She instantly pulled it away in pain.

—You're giving off current, Señor Clot!

—It's the static electricity, I can't help it.

They went pedalling off towards Castelló 13, Fernando's house.

ERNANDO RECEIVED US playing the part of a 'famous scientist meditating on the mystery of existence'. Indecent, he seemed to me. He was wearing a grey woollen sweater without a shirt underneath, jeans and shoes with the laces undone. He considered himself to be in possession of so exuberant an inner life that he was experiencing difficulty in preventing it from manifesting itself on the outside, too: it showed on his face, in the uncombed fringe and the two-day beard trimmed with nail scissors.

He'd got what had been our married home into such a state that I felt sorry for Beatriz, his assistant. On the dining table were various computers. On the shelf above the telly, a plastic bag with the logo of a department store. In full view on the little table, a bra. I couldn't help noticing the capacious size of the cups.

Neither could Clot's secretary.

Such volume immediately put me in mind of Inspector Menéndez and her shining eyes, and made me imagine with sadness the monotonous recreational activities of a separated husband.

We sat down in the lounge. Fernando, in his easy chair; Clot and the secretary on the sofa, from which they had to remove a dirty vest and two newspapers with the photo of my ex on the front page; Benito and me on reversed dining-room chairs with the back against our chests, in the interrogative position.

Clot expressed his condolences and excused himself: he needed to ask a few questions.

—I thought the case was closed, protested Fernando. The police have informed me of that.

On saying it he looked towards the XXL-size bra with an unnecessary and deliberate smile.

The secretary shot him a resentful look of annoyance.

—Not completely, not completely, Clot assured him. There're a few loose ends to tie up.

Fernando assured him he understood.

The first of the questions was whether we were separated.

—Only temporarily. I need to be on my own during certain periods in the process of scientific creation, he lied.

—But did you remain in touch?

—Of course.

—When was the last time you saw her?

—That same Wednesday, the night before her death, we had dinner together.

That, on the other hand, was true. He described the dinner in Estanis's house and explained that we'd gone for a drink afterwards to El Acme in Malasaña.

—Estanislao Pérez Ugena? Clot asked.

—The same. He's a personal friend, as well as being manager of the clinic.

'Personal friend'? Just how far was my dear Fer, my pitiful Fer, going to go in his descent into hell? He was now talking like journalists do and apparently he must also have had some impersonal friends, nice pets perhaps, holograms, properties, limited companies or identikit portraits.

—I left at around one thirty. Lola stayed behind to have another with some friends. After removing his hand from his fringe he looked inconsolably at the detective. —I never saw her alive again.

—Hang on a minute, Fernando! Tell them about Johnson! Why don't you mention anything about Johnson! It's the most important thing!

—Don't strain yourself, Teach, they don't hear you.

—It's just that he's hiding information, Viruta.

Fernando declared that he could think of no reason why someone might want to kill me. Clot informed him that they'd almost ruled out robbery as a motive. He asked Fernando whether he'd missed anything in what he called 'my studio'.

—I still haven't plucked up the courage to go and see it. I'll go tomorrow. My duty now is to attend to my parents-in-law.

I gave a start: when he went to my flat he'd find the manuscript of *All the More Reason*, the third appearance of the ingenious Cyclops, Benito Viruta, a synoptic chart of our wayward marriage.

—Dr Eguilaz, you investigate the essence of life, isn't that right? Clot asked all of a sudden.

—We can call it that, in a sense.

—I've heard you say on the telly that the aim of your investigations is to defeat death, is that true?

—Yes, but it's only a poetic truth, my friend. For the moment what we seek is to prolong life. Some day we will manage to defeat death, of that you may be sure, but I'm afraid that day is still a long way away.

—So it isn't possible to defeat death, Doc?

Fernando laughed.

—As yet, no, my friend. At the present time I only know one way to defeat death: the memory we leave behind in others.

—Fame? Are you referring to fame?

—Yes, of course, fame. Memory outlives death.

—And the green capsules? asked Clot, somewhat beside the point.

As if he'd heard an explosion Fernando went pale, directed his eyes towards the television shelf, cleared his throat and finally replied:

—And what have the green capsules got to do with it, Mr Clot? Of them I know what everyone else knows: that they're illegal and their formula is secret. It's what dealers use to punish addicts with, but nobody knows what they're made from.

—It was just a thought, said Clot, instantly changing the subject. —What kind of life did your wife lead, what were her habits?

What would Fernando know about it? He claimed I was a solitary person, reserved, a night bird and with irregular habits. He might as well have said I was acrobatic, an early riser and keen on stamp collecting. He pretended to suddenly remember a friend of mine, Marisol Mateos, the publisher of my books, an old chum from school. In answer to Clot's questions he had to admit I didn't move in criminal circles.

—This has to be a mistake, Fernando claimed, letting his fringe fall over his bulging eyes.

—When you left the bar, how did your wife look? Had she drunk a lot? Was she relaxed? Restless, perhaps? Did she show signs of being worried?

According to Fernando I'd had a couple of drinks, nothing excessive, and he saw me neither restless nor preoccupied.

—Who did she stay there with?

He cited Eduardo Sandoval, lyric poet, and Mario Navalón, literary critic, but once again he forgot to mention Johnson.

—Mr Clot, my parents-in-law await me. I must be at their side at such a painful time, if you'll excuse me.

—Naturally, amigo, of course. Do your duty, *sí, señor.*

They said goodbye. Fernando remained stretched out on the sofa with his feet on top of the table, looking up at the ceiling as if he were meditating.

M<small>Y LAST DINNER</small>, the night before they killed me, was one of those soporific reunions in the armour-plated villa of Estanislao Pérez Ugena, the famous captain of industry, a guy I felt sorry for because I never forgot that the poor sod had had to go through childhood and early life calling himself Estanislao.

Shortly before, I'd heard him on the radio and he'd reminded me of those two shops in Alberto Aguilera, Armchair World and Sofa-Bed Universe. As if they'd got him started on a favourite subject, all he did was go on about the world of politics, the world of the university, the world of journalism – it was like an isolated chapter by H.G. Wells, the war of the worlds! Or one of those novels with parallel universes and that Edwardian magic which reverses time and space. During the radio programme he claimed that he, Estanislao Pérez Ugena the businessman, kept in periodic touch with the world of culture.

Now I get it! Those dinners were just that: a catering service, his 'world of culture' delivered to his door, in case there was an emergency and it became indispensable to quote Machado in some

Administration Council meeting. Moreover, Estanis provided Scotch and duck breast ham, because it's obvious he reserved the Jabugo* and the single malts for those other worlds in which signs of intelligent life might already have been discovered: the bank, the tax-evasion consultants, the golf club.

I accepted, although I imagined the major attraction of the reunion was to see my ex and me together and to confirm how civilised and friendly our separation was.

Estanis seemed ten years younger than the rest of us. Unlike my father, he'd indeed managed to be in the right place at the right time. Instead of remaining with our elliptical generation, he'd hooked up with an older one (along with Fernando) in order to occupy what they themselves called 'the resources of power'.

In the eighties he'd adopted the behaviour of an atom executive and become spartan, athletic and almost completely herbivorous. He spoke perfect Anglo, without a trace of a Spanish accent, and had acquired a small fortune through the rezoning of rural land for the development of an industrial estate. Afterwards, he'd invested in the pharmaceutical sector, with UgePharma, and was also the owner of more than fifty per cent of the clinic.

Like some beetles, he'd modified his features with the passing of time adapting them to the predatory and parasitic life. His mandibles had grown and now never completely fitted one into the other, and he'd acquired a patrician's head with greying temples and half-frame glasses. Once I saw him barefoot and his pointed toenails were still ingrowing. What's more, the swollen ankles and

---

*The area north-west of Seville and close to the Portuguese border where Spain's best ham comes from.

varicose-veined legs betrayed his lowly origins, however much the gold cufflinks, silk tie and starched shirt collar might announce his manifest destiny in various Administration Councils.

Of the sinister years when he'd carried a knife in his pocket, he preserved only the telephone number of a few delinquents he'd known at the time, when he was still banging tables with his fist and securing his wallet with a thick elastic band.

They might come in useful, as he was wont to repeat.

You never know, as my mother would say.

After we said goodbye to Estanis we went for a drink in Malasaña on the other side of the Castellana Canal, on the Rive Gauche, Eduardo, Mario Navalón, Fernando and me.

That was where we met up with Johnson.

—Teach, Teach, watch out, this one's stirring! Benito suddenly informed me.

Fernando had decided he'd meditated for long enough in the same position, stretched out on the sofa, with his feet on top of the table, building castles in the air. He called my parents to confirm he was heading for their place. We went down with him in the lift.

—Cor! The detective and the girl are hidden over there, Benito pointed out.

Fernando didn't see them.

Clot and his secretary were crouching, sheltered behind some dustbins. The girl was clutching her skirt in order to cover her thighs.

—Thank goodness, Benito, Clot didn't believe a word of what Fernando said either.

I was beginning to trust that Clot fellow or perhaps, like my father, I was on the point of totally losing my judgement.

It surprised me the detective had mentioned fame.

He'd hit the nail on the head, maybe by chance, since fame was the only thing that really interested my ex-husband.

—You don't mess around with fame, Fernando was in the habit of saying.

Eduardo Sandoval had told Fernando one day that he was once eating with his parents in a restaurant and at the next table was Lola Flores. Twenty years afterwards Eduardito, the lyric poet, still remembered how La Faraona was dressed, what she ate (macaroni, a grilled steak with salad and home-made crème caramel) and even the earrings she had on, two pearls that went on gleaming in the darkness of the memory of the whole Sandoval family.

On another occasion Fernando's parents had gone to dinner in the house of some friends in Torres Blancas on the Avenida de América. In the porch Fernando's mother had said:

—Ooh, it's pitch black here!

A booming voice resonated in the dark:

—Señora, how do you expect to see if you don't turn on the light!

It was Camilo José Cela, banging the switch with his fist.

This must have occurred in the seventies and subsequently every time the name of the corpulent, prize-winning writer came up in conversation Fernando's mother came over all cutting:

—That man is a real lout, and she repeated over and again the remote anecdote of her encounter with the author of *The Beehive*.

Fernando himself had never forgotten the day he'd seen Kiko Ledgard in the middle of Calle Zurburán, years after he'd stopped appearing on the telly. He who had been the famous presenter of

Un, Dos, Tres went up to Fernando to ask him where Calle García de Paredes was.

All through his life Fernando had remembered that instant as if he were reliving it. He forgot his mother's last words, the details of his first fuck, the sensation of waking in a hospital bed when they operated on him for appendicitis, but never the impression it produced in him seeing Kiko Ledgard, who'd been years without appearing anywhere, in person. As a kid they'd given Fernando a photo signed by Kiko himself and, upon recognising him in Calle Zurburán, his whole body trembled, as if there'd been an unexpected change of temperature.

Kiko manifested a Machado-like dejection. He was walking alone, sad, tired, pensive and old. He'd got lost two blocks from the street he was looking for. He was wearing grey flannel trousers, a red polo-necked sweater and a check jacket. And, of course, as Fernando remembered with precision, a watch on both wrists and socks of different colours: one red and the other blue.

There was no point coming to Fernando with that old guff: fame was a perfectly serious matter.

As he saw it, every one of the most anodyne acts of a famous person, without the famous person realising it, indelibly marked the life of the anonymous unknowns whose paths he or she crossed. The anonymous pedestrians had no other option but to remember it for evermore, for evermore! Never in all their anonymous lives would it be erased from their memory. They would recount it to friends and family: I dined one day right next to Lola Flores, I saw Cela on a porch, Kiko Ledgard asked me something in the street.

—For evermore! repeated Fernando, as if he were Edgar Allan Poe's raven. Can you imagine it, Lola? Can you imagine forming part of the memory of people you don't know, of the things parents tell their children, of something which is handed down from generation to generation and lasts for ever?

Eduardo Sandoval, for instance, seemed to seriously think there was a very special relationship between his family and Lola Flores. When the singer died we all asked ourselves whether we shouldn't offer him our condolences.

—Actually, she was a very simple person, began the poet, deeply affected, and he went back to telling us about the macaroni, grilled steak with salad and the home-made crème caramel, on the table next door, just as I'm seeing you now.

Fernando's mother, on the other hand, always felt an antipathy towards Cela which the passing of the years and all the decorations did nothing to allay, a livelier and more intense feeling than those she felt for most of the members of her own family. Every time Cela received a literary prize, the good woman felt obliged to explain her position:

—I'm sorry, I'm happy for him, but it has to be said he's a very coarse man. A great writer, that I don't dispute, but an ill-mannered fellow. And there appeared, intact, rescued from oblivion, the story of that encounter in the darkened porch in Torres Blancas.

Fernando himself was convinced he understood the singular and sombre destiny of Kiko Ledgard better than anyone, the feeling of shame of having been someone and the pain of no longer being that person, his stubbornness in wearing two watches, different coloured socks; in short, the enigmatic and endless tragedy that was his life... and this is as far as I go!

On any one day, without doing a thing, just by going out on to the street, Lola de España, CJC or Kiki Ledgard could imprint themselves on other people's memories, mark the lives of hundreds of anonymous strangers for all time, remain intact in the face of death and oblivion.

Was I imagining it? Did I maybe think it was some kind of game? To be taken lightly? Was fame superficial? Was the desire to be famous frivolous?

I saw Fernando happy only when he was a candidate for the Nobel for the first time, thanks to those researches my father had paved the way with (with no way forward and no way back, as he confessed to us afterwards).

From that moment on Fernando could at last give hundreds of interviews in which to finally repeat that he detested fame.

By then I'd already decided to leave. To him, as it happened, it didn't matter too much. He wanted only to endure in the future memory of strangers: to be immortal through the Nobel Prize.

For Fernando fame must have been like shooting up with heroin. Something it was also seemingly worth giving up your life for a perfectly serious matter, as it was for Carlos Viloria.

On one occasion Carlos had tried to explain it to me. We were in his studio flat on Calle San Marcos, next to Plaza de Chueca. Cati had gone off to score.

By that time Carlos's intimate relationship with needles was no longer a secret, we all knew he was making his way along that other path with no way forward and no way back.

We were drinking gin mixed with tap water and freshly squeezed lemon. Carlos was shivering, as if he were extremely cold.

—Have you ever gone walking at night on your own, in no particular direction, freezing with cold, and there's nowhere to go? he asked me. You're a long way from home, you don't even know where you are, they've closed the metro, there's not a soul about, there're no bars open. It's one of those nightmarish nights, with the wind lashing your face, you keep treading in puddles, everything's dark and your throat's sore. You plunge desperately onwards and suddenly, from the pavement, you see a light go on above you, a window with a welcoming light, yellowish and warm. You look inside from the street, you fix your eyes on that light, like a moth, and all you think is how much you'd like to be inside, on the other side of that window. It makes you want to cry. Well, now imagine you could be on the other side of that pane of glass, Lola, imagine it, OK? If you wish it, you're already inside and what's more it's your house, your own house. Imagine it. Through the art of magic, as Eduardito would say. But not only that, it's better yet: it's your house, you're three years old and you end up sleeping in the arms of your mother. Can you imagine it, Lola. Do you get the idea?

That was what Carlos had tried to explain to me. A fix made him feel safe, but not only from the cold of night, from the puddles of rainwater, the wind in the face and the black waters of the Castellana Canal. Safer still: safe from life, like sleeping children, safe from the past and the future, safe from himself. As if he could be three years old again and asleep in his mother's arms, as if he could pass to the other side, get behind the pane of glass.

—It's impossible to explain, it's not something you can imagine, you have to live it, added Carlos, and looked at his hands.

He was sitting shivering on the sofa, impatiently awaiting the little packet of smack. He had such a helpless look I wanted to hug him and give him warmth, although I already knew the cold he was feeling came from within himself: only the smack could get rid of it, also from inside, by travelling through his veins the way the roots of a tree do through the earth.

I can still hum the Velvet's 'Heroin'. I remember Carlos, Cati, both of them dead, cold ashes on the other side of the glass pane, locked out of themselves, like when you leave your keys indoors and you remain locked out, because the rest of the world is within reach but what does it matter if you now can't get back into your own house.

Was fame the only thing that could make Fernando feel warm? Was it his heroin? Was he capable of anything to get it? Of killing? Of killing me, too?

When Cati arrived, Carlos opened her bag and took out a penknife and a syringe. He unwrapped the silver paper and cut off a little piece with the knife. He put it in a teaspoon. He measured water with the syringe and squirted it into the spoon, which he then heated with the lighter in order to dissolve the brown powder.

I drew close in silence.

He rested the needle on the spoon, put a tiny ball of cotton wool on the point and pulled the plunger to absorb it all. With a handkerchief he made a tourniquet a little above his left elbow. He stuck the needle in a vein. First he pulled the plunger back and I saw a string of blood describe a red flower inside the cylinder, the labyrinth of a rose that opens. Then he pressed the plunger all the way in and closed his eyes. He sighed. To me it seemed as if he'd ended up untying a very tight knot. He loosened the handkerchief and withdrew the syringe.

He was immobile, his eyes closed.

I took a glass of tap water and drank it in one go, my throat was hurting and my voice wouldn't come.

I didn't dare say anything to him.

Or to look at that needle, stained with Carlos's blood.

Twenty minutes must have gone by. The clouds were swirling about towards the west, from Calle Almirante, banging into the aerials on the roofs, against which they were getting shredded.

All of a sudden Carlos looked my way.

—It frightens you, doesn't it?

His eyes were a deadened blue, almost grey.

—Yes, a bit, I replied without thinking, saying the first thing that came into my head.

He smiled.

I corrected myself.

—Frightened, no, Carlos. I don't like needles, that's all.

—Sure, Lola, sure. Just like everybody. It isn't the heroin, it's the needles, right?

When I went out into the street it was drizzling. Without my glasses on, the city was all misshapen, the traffic lights formed pools of colour and the front lamps of the bikes rivers of light that flowed into the black water of the Castellana Canal.

That was the last thing Carlos did in his life, see that blood rose open before falling asleep in the arms of his mother.

Safe for ever, as if he were alive for ever, as if he'd also defeated death.

Is it possible to defeat death? Tell me, Carlos. Tell me, Fernando. Have you managed it?

After removing the safety chain, spied on by Clot, by the secretary and by us, Fernando got on his bike, a latest-model Orbea with streamlining in different greys, and set off for my parents' house, pedalling unhurriedly.

Then Clot made a sign to the secretary and they tiptoed up the stairs.

The detective opened the door effortlessly with a Swiss Army knife.

They slipped into Fernando's flat.

—Let's see what you've learnt, Suzie-Kay: the man was hiding information, that much is clear, but I reckon he was also hiding an object. Where would you say it is?

—In the toilet cistern?

—Negative and forget it.

—I've got it! Inside the oven?

—No way, Little Suzie. It's obvious, it's in the only place the guy didn't look at once, except when I asked him about the green capsules. And as always we'll find it right in front of our eyes I'm sure.

—On top of the telly?

—Bingo! You're learning.

Clot patted her shoulder and the secretary gave a start.

—You're giving off static, boss!

Charlie Clot made for the shelf and opened the plastic bag that was on top of the telly.

Inside was the black folder Johnson had entrusted to me, the same one I gave to the two henchmen, Brains and the Boss, the one that had cost me my life.

He photographed the papers it contained, put everything back the way it was, and he and that Suzie Koebnick person left the building without anyone seeing them.

—Gordon Bennett! So it was your husband! Benito declared.

—My ex-husband, kid, my ex-husband.

—Life's little ups and downs!

Yeah, some ups and downs…

Small change.

We leave home all happy, the big bucks in our mitts, all nice and warm, and in the end life gives us back a few worthless cents.

We adults always end up scrabbling around for small change, it's all we have left, although we might not even remember now where or when we've changed those banknotes we had as youngsters, upon leaving home. To life, this life, you hand over freshly minted paper money and afterwards it gives you back nothing but loose change, infinitesimal fractions, nickels and dimes, those coins that wear the bottom out of your pockets and dirty your fingers.

A miserly life that's forever light-fingered when giving change, as we know, but it's all the same to us. We're not going to worry ourselves about checking the change, either. You have to live until the last banknote is spent, without reckoning up on your fingers, so as to leave with your head held high and saying, Keep the change!

Maybe that way we might be deserving of the satisfaction of hearing life cry out behind our backs, so that all those at the bar can hear: Jaaaackpoooot!

—I'm dead surprised, I swear… Your own ex-husband, Teach!

—That's the way things go, kid.

It's true, events are happy to take an unexpected turn, perhaps with the sole purpose of leaving us in the dark, so to speak.

With me, however, they didn't manage it.

I knew it.

Ever since Inspector Menéndez pronounced the statistical truth, I'd managed to admit to the emotional one: Fernando may have been the person responsible for my death.

I knew it but still didn't want to believe it, not even on seeing the documents hidden in his house.

Had Fernando been the one who'd arranged my execution at the hands of the Boss and Brains? The one who'd given instructions from the other end of the telephone?

It could be, why not? The statistics demonstrate it but I didn't want to believe it, doubtless in order to protect myself, in order not to do myself too much harm, in order not to have to draw too many conclusions.

WE SPEND HALF OUR LIVES banging into furniture, getting our fingers trapped in doors, bumping against the sharp corner of tables. The day arrives, however, when you bend down to get a pan and on standing up you hit your head on the door of the glasses cupboard. If the first thing you think is it's your husband's fault, that he's left it open again, then the marriage is already dead, the love's evaporated and there's nothing to be done.

The day a woman no longer says 'Bloody door!' but 'What a bastard!' it's all over.

Now it's not the bloody door you've banged into but your entire life, your life which is badly closed, which is where it shouldn't be, lying in wait, prepared to whack you on the forehead. 'Bloody life!', that's what a woman thinks, because the problem isn't the cupboard that oughtn't to have been open but the life you lead, which shouldn't be there, lying across the middle of your path.

There's nothing you can do about it, you have to slam the door.

From that moment on, the first thing you find of a morning is a cigarette butt floating in the toilet bowl. The coffee spoon staining the worktop. Dirty clothes in the bidet. Shoes all over the floor. Just like always, sure, but before you didn't notice it. Now, on the other hand, you see nothing else and time and again you bang into your own body, which is blocking the way.

You ask yourself what's happened. Has he changed? Have you changed? Have the two of you gone your own separate ways? What was the Fernando I married like, the man I loved, the man who loved me? Was it all a lie, then? How did we get to this point?

There are no reasons or they're the same reasons that have turned around without being seen and lain face down. What I liked so much before was the same thing I was later unable to stand. At first I loved seeing Fernando when he thought I wasn't looking at him, concentrating on his work; his way of dressing, always in dark colours, impressed me; the way he ate so fast amused me. A few years later I could no longer stand his way of concentrating while he hummed the same song over and over again, his ash-coloured clothes and the fact that he devoured his food without chewing it. As simple as that.

I got to thinking it makes no difference, that love is pure make it up as you go along, do-it-yourself, that you're the one who creates everything with your own hands and uses the same reasons for loving and for stopping loving, a single device that works just as well for screwing and unscrewing.

We got married nine months after the death of Carlos.

While he was alive I always thought there was a possibility Carlos Viloria would fall in love with me, however remote it might be.

Fernando and I almost always went out together. We used to begin in the Little Crab on Calle Apodaca, drinking beer from the barrel. They put the beer in clay mugs you were meant to call 'bocks'. From there we wheeled along to Malasaña, where every night we repeated a similar itinerary: three 103s in El Sol, another two in La Rosa or El Morgenstern, glasses of fizzy pop at the bars of the Hermanos Otero or El Muguruza and sometimes a hard-boiled egg with paprika or one of those sandwiches they sell on the pavement on folding tables. They prepare them with herbs from plant pots, but call them whole food and claim they're therapeutic.

One day, walking down streets without paving stones, we came out in the Plaza de San Idefonso, a quadrilateral of concrete on to which the light of the moon was spilling and to where there reached, every three and a half minutes, the beam of the Puerto Atocha lighthouse.

Without realising it we were going along hand in hand.

Fernando suggested we went to his house.

I said yes without knowing why. I'm beyond hope, that's how my life was, I always obeyed, filled in diaries, remained frozen at the request of a naked man...

In the lift, looking at ourselves in the mirror, we saw that other couple who were ascending in an embrace to go to bed.

The two of us suddenly felt like actors on a stage, performing a play. We knew the text, knew what we had to say, what we had to do, but we no longer found meaning or interest in it, it was as if it was only happening to the other two, the ones in the mirror.

As they say in the theatre: the show must go on.

Both of us pretended we were fulfilling our desires.

Maybe we desired to believe it.

So sex is magical, Eduardito, my friend?

Yes, very magical. To what was Eduardito referring? To the

fact that it made things disappear? Changed some things for other things? Was the hand always quicker than the eye? Did the other person know, without you saying anything, which card you'd hidden? Was the coin never where you'd seen it? Does it put the artiste's life in danger, perhaps?

Yes, Eduardo, dear: hocus-pocus.

Fernando asked me to marry him.

I obeyed because I'm a hopeless case.

In the meantime the manuscript Carlos was clutching when he died, *Profound Deafness*, published after his death, became an instant classic, 'the critical conscience of the century', as the papers said.

A week after our wedding Cati turned up a corpse.

They found her hanging from a cornice of the Telefónica skyscraper, swinging from side to side above Gran Vía like a hypnotist's pendulum.

She was one of the first victims of the green capsules. They say they cause such unbearable nightmares to those who use them that they die of fright. Of fright, no more, no less.

Once dead, they'd extracted an eye and she had her tongue and various fingers and toes amputated. It was the law of the drug dealers, the lesson that then became a classic for those who moved the stuff on their own account.

It was around that time that my father quit the clinic. Fernando took over his position and I thought he was going to burst with happiness, but it was from that moment on that he too began going downhill.

A pencil with the lead broken inside, like my father.

Fernando needed somebody to blame. I was somebody and I was at hand.

One day I said to him:

—I'm not happy, Fernando.

We were talking less and less, so I had to profit from the moment we were getting ready to go to the launch of the first book by Mario Navalón, the literary critic: *The Use of Onomatopoeia During the Reading of Juan Benet.*

The event half an hour away was a guarantee that the conversation couldn't go on for long and end up in an argument.

We went on sharing the bathroom without any sense of shame, without any complicity and almost without looking at each other. While Fer was shaving, I was painting my toenails with red varnish, sitting on the toilet.

I was going to put on a dress with a plunging neckline.

I remember it well, it was an obstinate, belligerent spring, there were wild flowers in the irrigation ditches around the acacias, geraniums on the balconies, carnivorous plants were growing in ministry vases, privet was budding unexpectedly in the round plazas and by night the mechanical ducks on Mariano de Cavia were swimming in the fountain, agitating their wings and splashing those who kept late hours. During the day, the shadows of birds in flight crossed the pavements like swift insects; sparrows hopped, frame by frame, looking for breadcrumbs until their beaks got stuck in a bit of chewing gum; and allergic people sneezed ceaselessly, with exaggerated violence, so as to be able to find a subject of conversation.

The event was in the Ateneo and I was going to go in red sandals and that dress which looked like an open balcony. Fernando splashed hot water on his face and shook the canister of foam with unnecessary violence. I placed my right foot on the edge of the bidet and began putting wads of cotton wool between my toes. That was when I said I wasn't happy.

My husband seemed to feel truly glad:

—Sure, *mujer*, very good! There's no bloody need to be.

—Don't talk daft, Fer.

Happiness? Fernando was incapable of imagining it. But what had I believed? That we were in a Walt Disney movie?

—All that stuff about happiness is rubbish. Don't go deceiving yourself, what I want is to find the secret of life… Next to that, happiness is a mere trifle, he confessed to me, wrinkling up his nose as if he were gazing upon small tradesmen, grocers in blue coats or a gathering of civil servants with their yellow souls, each one doubled over in his own cupboard with his corresponding mothball.

In order to stretch the skin of his cheeks he was twisting his mouth with vehement gestures, as if he were drowning or I were seeing him through the spyhole of a door.

To Fernando, wanting to be happy seemed a contradiction. He was like those communist impresarios, great advocates of equality, am I right? Long Live the Revolution, sure, but only as long as they could go on being cocooned in their class privileges. How was he, a famous brain researcher, going to be in favour of happiness, just as if he were a contestant or like the announcers on the telly!

—No, if seen that way.

—Life is serious, Lola. Your father knew it.

—My father chose to be happy.

—He got scared, Lola, I'm sorry to have to tell you. Your father was afraid. He didn't want to go on.

It wasn't the first time he'd insinuated that my father, when he was on the point of discovering the secret of life, neuroprotein K666, had stepped back.

What my father said is that this was a path with no way forward and no way back.

Fernando took his place.

—You wouldn't renounce being happy, then, as long as you could defeat death? he insisted.

—I suppose so, I said, convinced of the opposite.

As I go on being convinced, now too, from here, on the other side.

—So there you have it, Lola.

I said yes in order not to argue and reminded him it was time to go to the Ateneo.

We arrived at the event very unhappy.

Some more than others, of course.

Fernando was openly tormented. His unhappiness was so visible it made other people uncomfortable, especially me. Being at his side was like looking at someone cross-eyed, talking to a stutterer or walking with a cripple.

Our marriage went on that way, heading towards the Palaeolithic, to non-verbal communication, almost by signs, territorial rivalries and with turns guarding the fire, for if it went out we'd no longer know how to relight it.

I wanted to be happy.

One day I banged my forehead on the cupboard door, blood flowed and I saw stars.

—Bloody life! I cried.

In the bathroom I dabbed on Mercurochrome and looked at myself in the mirror.

I suddenly thought that on the other side of the wall, behind the black spot where the silvering had come off, there could be someone watching me. I turned on the tap and let the water run. Who was out there, watching me live? Maybe my parents, who were always repeating that if only they could see me through a tiny little hole, like the one in the mirror? An unknown god? The future readers of those Benito Viruta books I'd started publishing?

I needed someone who'd watch my life from close to. If there was nobody to see me live, nobody who'd pay attention, I'd disappear, evaporate, end up misting up the mirror without a finger writing my name in the steam.

We all need someone who knows our bones one by one. Someone who knows everything, who's had access to the content of our hearts. Someone who's been a witness to our suffering, the undeserved pain, the wasted effort.

Yes, but let's be sincere: we also need the opposite. We need to trust in the fact that there's no one who really does know all our bones. That no one can look at us against the light or under the carpet. That no one knows the truth of our heart.

That's the way we are, as Eduardo used to say in school, tightrope walkers, forever balancing unsteadily between two inhuman abysses, the two desires that cannot be fulfilled at the same time.

I turned off the tap, slammed the door and left the house.

Have I been happy?

In fact, why do we still speak of 'unhappiness', 'dissatisfaction' or 'discontentment'? As if we knew all too well what happiness, satisfaction and contentment were; as if we could only imagine their opposites by adding a negative prefix; as if unhappiness were no more than a working hypothesis, a conjecture typical of visionaries that can only be conceived through the negation of what we all know and experience on a daily basis: happiness, satisfaction, contentment.

Well, some contentment.

We're like exiles, banished from a country we don't remember, like the kids on the back row, those repeating-a-year types who've been chucked out of some other school, a place where happiness must have been the only thing we knew, since there we didn't even have the words to name its absence. We remember nothing, yet fossils in the language still remain, like the chewing gum stuck on the inside of your pocket or the ink of that bust pen that no longer writes but still stains your fingers and clothes.

Our mother tongue, Spanish, the forbidden lingo, is that shadow of paradise which darkens our smile and reminds us we're foreigners, expelled from the school of happiness, condemned to yearn for something we don't even remember.

Have I been happy? What difference does it make…

Happiness has to be like our holiday photos: we can only see it when we finally take them to be developed, a long time afterwards, in autumn.

That's how we must live, saying to the others, 'Position yourself so I can do your photo, I've got to finish the film.' We photograph unknown people only to be able to see the snap of that night on which we were happy. And we also position ourselves unhesitatingly before other people's cameras so they can take images of their loved ones to be developed.

In the end, to finish the roll, we've been shooting photos haphazardly, blurred sunsets, buildings on a slant, out-of-focus faces. What a life. How many bad times, how much suffering and how many sad Sunday afternoons we have to photograph in order to be able to develop that reel in which we appear smiling in a single photo. Just how many images of unknown people, of nameless streets, of blurred landscapes have we needed?

And on top of that, when we open the yellow envelope from the chemist's, it transpires that the ones that were going to turn out so well never do: a man walked in front, the branch of a tree hides a face, eyes are reddened by the flash.

On the other hand, will that unexpected photo appear which demonstrates that one day we were happy without even knowing it? That photo nobody remembers taking, where we were, who's the man by our side hugging us.

Question: why didn't we realise it at the time?

Answer: because we don't know how to be happy on purpose, we're only good at finding what we weren't looking for.

Is that photo in black and white with my father, in which I still don't know why I was crying, the one that's now on top of my corpse under the earth, maybe the only one that's come out of my happiness?

I sat in silence in the lounge of that house I'd fled from years before, slamming the door, at Castelló 13, where the papers that had cost me my life were, while Benito asked me time and again if I felt all right and I got to thinking about making him face the wall as a punishment, just so the insufferable kid would leave me in peace.

WHEN CLOT AND HIS SECRETARY went off, Benito and I remained in Fernando's house. After a couple of hours Fernando came back accompanied by Estanis Pérez Ugena, who'd apparently been waiting for him in the bar below.

Fernando handed him the bag with the file in it. After examining the papers Estanis nodded his head.

—Correct. It's all here. Without even knowing it, that idiot Johnson had stolen a bomb. Dynamite. Here's your Nobel Prize at last, Fer, he said, handing him one of the documents.

—Old Eguíbar's neuroprotein.

That had to be my father. My legs trembled.

—The rest I'm going to destroy and end of story. What gives, Fernando?

—I don't know. You tell me. Something's up, Estanis.

Estanis took a seat. Fernando stayed on his feet, leaning against the bookcase.

—Out with it, old chap.

—A detective's been asking questions. He asked about the green capsules.

—A cop?

—No, a snoop, a private eye. My father-in-law's hired him.

Estanis breathed noisily, rubbed his eyes behind his glasses, and took a caramel from his pocket. Fernando, meanwhile, lit a cigarette.

—Stubborn old fool! Poor idiot, he can't resign himself to the disappearance of María Dolores. The sleuth'll have heard whispers, there's nothing to worry about. Tell me who the flatfoot is and I'll take care of things.

—Charles Clot, that's the name.

—Charlie Clot! Estanis expressed his surprise by slapping a thigh.

—Who is he?

—An old story. Clot got hold of that same bit of paper before Johnson stole it, the formula for the green capsules, but also the basis for synthesising the neuroprotein.

—It's not possible, Estanis. Clot knows everything, then! Fernando seemed scared.

—Everything's OK, don't let it get to you. Estanis crunched the caramel between his teeth. —Man Chopeitia saw to the business himself.

—I want to know what's happening.

—The green capsules cause the death of addicts with inhuman suffering, but they also have beneficial effects on damaged brains: Parkinson's, Alzheimer's.

—Tell me something I don't know, brother. You're talking about neuroprotein K666 and about my Nobel Prize.

In profile, Fernando's protruding eyes and pointed nose gave him a look somewhere between vehement and numismatic.

—Clot has a daughter with cerebral palsy, Estanis said. —When he got hold of the formula for the green capsules, he negotiated with Manex Chopeitia. The paper in exchange for secret medication for his daughter. As you'll see, we've got him by the short and curlies: if we cut off the supply, his daughter'll turn into a vegetable. I don't think that's of interest to him.

—Are you sure of what you're saying?

—Fernando, please! That's what they pay me for: to know things. That's my job: taking decisions. Forget about the whole thing. Haven't you got what you wanted?

—I have what I wanted. Also something I didn't want: Lola's death.

—That was inevitable, Fer. Think no more about it. Go and publish your discovery and win the Nobel. I'll take care of old Clot.

—Agreed.

Estanis patted him on the shoulder and before leaving handed him a box of pills.

—Take two, sleep for a few hours and don't worry. You need it.

Alone, Ferando swallowed the capsules and lay down on the sofa.

—Are we going with Estanis to look for Clot? asked Viruta.

—Not now. I need to see this. We'll find the detective after.

We waited for my ex-husband to fall asleep.

Then his dream began rising like a cloud of smoke, adopting a triangular shape. I saw Estanis's office. I heard the mobile phone. Estanis took the call.

—That person knows too much, then: she'll have to be eliminated, he said.

Next I saw Fernando and Estanis talking. Daylight came in through the window.

—That was what happened. I never suspected it could be María Dolores, Estanis was saying.

—And it was necessary to eliminate her, is that it? As easy as that?

—I'm sorry, Fernando. That's the way it's happened.

—And if you'd known it was her? What then?

—I didn't know, I'm telling you for the last time. Calm down. They'll bring you the papers, it's safer.

In Fernando's dream, the scene was repeated time and again, until the phrase took on a special resonance: 'She knows too much, she'll have to be eliminated.'

Afterwards I saw the back of a woman who was making off towards the line of the horizon.

It was hard for me to recognise myself in Fernando's dream, because I didn't see my face, my pretty face.

I was walking energetically towards the horizon, which remained for ever at the same distance.

—This sure is good! the kid blurted out. —Now it turns out it wasn't your ex-husband, Teach. And neither is the other one to blame. It's not right! Who's the real baddie, Teach? Somebody has to bear the blame, no?

—Maybe Estanis lied to Fernando. Has that occurred to you, Benito? Maybe there are no baddies and goodies, but each person does what he can, Beni. Think about it.

He began to do so right there and then, half closing the eye without a patch.

Fernando wasn't to blame, then? Hadn't I been the innocent victim of my ex-husband's ambition? Or just like my father, was the problem, in short, that I was never in the right place at the right time?

—Here, there's nothing to be done. So let's be off.

—I was thinking, Teach, forgive me.

—Let's see if we find Clot.

I T WAS A FLASH OF LIGHTNING, we all saw it, Carlos Viloria lived zigzag-style; afterwards we stayed waiting, sure it'd be repeated, but blackness was all we saw, the opaque sky and some low clouds which advanced like a spreading puddle.

Later the birds flapped their wings and it was day: all had ended. The dawn wind pushed the swings in the Plaza de Chueca, chains creaked, beer cans and empty bottles rolled along the ground, the last drops of rain bounced off the kiddies' slide, the streetlights were about to go off and the metal blinds of the bars to go up: life went on and Carlos was dead.

On the radio Los Secretos were playing:

On a misty windowpane
I wrote your name
without realising it
and my eyes were just like that pane
thinking of her.
The paintings don't have colours.
The roses don't seem flowers,
There's no dawn chorus
Nothing's the same, nothing's the same,
Nothing's the same, nothing...

For a few months we were waiting for an explanation to emerge, something for us to get a hold of, a hot clue, a shipwrecked sailor's spar or that tree branch which grows at the edge of the cliff. We trusted in his papers, even in his famous unpublished novel, in an unexpected bit of news, a doctor's call, anything.

It hadn't been an accidental overdose, Carlos wanted to die, so there had to be something that would explain everything, a bit of information that he'd kept secret. That he'd tested positive in an Aids test, that he had cancer, that he was undergoing psychiatric treatment, that he was homosexual, anything.

We were in need of it.

But nothing appeared. There wasn't an explanation.

There never is.

I wanted to believe that Carlos didn't really want to kill himself. That it was only a cry for help, an accident or an error of judgement.

But it's not true, he wanted to kill himself.

He wanted to disappear. Or maybe he wanted the rest of the universe to disappear.

For all we know the world could be only inside our heads. He who presses the barrel of the gun to his temple fires against the whole universe. It has no meaning for him to send a goodbye letter because, as Nabokov said, he's going to make all the postmen on the planet instantly disappear.

A contract killer, the Boss or Brains, or whoever hired them – Fernando? Estanis? Both? – kills a single person. Me, in this instance, however strange it may seem, or even by mistake. Every suicide, meanwhile, commits genocide, exterminates the entire human species, annihilates the universe, destroys all that is not himself, from the postal service to that watch he's just wound up and the glasses he's left on the bedside table.

On bringing the needle to his arm Carlos had already decided in his heart to destroy the entire universe, to reject it in its entirety.

To reject me. Cati. Fernando. His parents. His unpublished novel. The possibility of going on reading Nabokov, Azorín or Nietzsche.

Benito and I were lucky. We found Clot in his office, developing the photos of the documents. When they were ready he put them in a file and went pedalling off on his long-suffering Orbea towards Antón Martín. He visited various cruddy bars, drank a lot of whisky and, when he got tired, went back home.

What Clot called 'home' was the same flat Carlos Viloria had lived in, that attic on Calle San Marcos I'd spent the night in during the invasion.

Clot hadn't even bothered to change the photos of writers Carlos had stuck on the wall.

There, in that flat the detective was now living in, someone must have left a window open that night because the wind blew, that *bufera infernal, che mai non resta*, a mistral that swept me into the air and dragged me along, the hurricane that separates lovers from other mortals, the one that makes them take off as if they were flocks of starlings and keeps them suspended, whipping them from side to side, without rest, without touching the ground, without ever looking down.

I fell in love with Carlos.

We'd been sweethearts as kids, in Alberchina, one summer. It lasted as long as did the transfers on our arms. But that didn't count, it wasn't the same.

Or was it? Or would it perhaps be the same movie refilmed with different sets, as Freud and my father maintained?

Before the invasion, I took to meeting Carlos in El Acme, in the intervals between his comings and goings that seemed mysterious to me then. Underfoot, there was sawdust, gambas peels, serviettes and used toothpicks. There were display units with Russian salad and croquettes. There were two tins of El Velero tuna, the size of small bike wheels, and other triangular ones of Cuca mussels. A painted tile I still remember by heart listed the six stages of drunkenness:

A readiness to speak
A glorification of friendship
Songs of home
A familiar way with authority
Insulting the clergy
Delirium tremens

On the other side of the bar a rectangular hatch communicated with the kitchen. A section of the cook was visible, from collarbone to hip, and we were able to contemplate the manoeuvres of her fat arms and her breasts, like butane canisters, wobbling over steaming pans. From there came the helpings of viscera and entrails Carlos liked, the fried chicken giblets, mesenteries or liver and onions, and from there came the frightened voice shouting:

—They're shooting in Congress, it's a *coup d'état*!

Silence descended on the bar and the complete cook appeared through the side door carrying a transistor with the volume turned up.

—It's '36 all over again! exclaimed a scared little man standing on a stool.

A queue formed to call home on the phone.

Carlos took me by the hand and I closed my eyes.

The cook took off her apron and rushed out into the street. She was going to buy provisions, packets of rice, bags of sliced bread, tins of sardines, the same things our mothers purchased when Carrero Blanco flew over Madrid riding in his Dodge Dart and they had to come and pick us up from school.

—Go to your house, Carlos said. —Your parents'll be worried.

—My parents are in Alberchina, it's all the same to me. What're you going to do?

—Nothing, mine are in Alberchina, too.

We stayed in El Acme, which didn't close; there, nobody seemed to have a family, loved ones, no light kept on in the window.

We drank red wine.

At midnight the king appeared on the telly with a uniform like a little lead soldier's.

—We're saved, stated the cook, who was arranging the assembled provisions behind the bar.

—The Americans have saved us. They're going to strengthen democracy, opined the waiter.

—The king's bottled out, affirmed Don Baldomero, the diminutive man atop the stool. —It's been her, as in all marriages. She'll have fired off an ultimatum by Zimmerman Telegram:* 'Juanito, stop, do what you want, stop, but if you make the coup,

---

*A coded telegram sent by German Foreign Secretary Arthur Zimmermann on 16 January 1917 to the German ambassador in Mexico, Heinrich von Eckardt, at the height of the First World War encouraging him to arrange a military alliance between Germany and Mexico against the USA. The telegram was intercepted and decoded by the British; its contents hastened the USA's entry into the war.

stop, I'm leaving with the kids and here you stay, stop, you'll know what's best for you, stop and end of message.'

—Do you think the king was in on it, Don Baldo? asked the cook.

—Don't be naive, Doña Teresa. General Armada* wouldn't lift a finger without relying on the king, I can assure you. The fact is the queen's smart and what's more she's got a memory, something that's been renounced here by an absolute majority. She knows only too well what happens to kings when they support military uprisings, like in Greece. Look, in this country nobody remembers anything, we start from scratch time and again.

—Yes, but now with the Americans. Now this is going to get serious, insisted the waiter.

—Listen, Don Baldo, what if the king's gone on the telly to stop the coup?

—It's about time! protested Don Baldomero, tapping the face of his watch with the tip of his index finger. —Now you'll see, gentlemen, we're going to restore order, yes of course, but on the basis of a doubt, take care now, on a doubt. What can grow when it's rooted in doubt? And if not, let time be the judge.

—No way, Don Baldo, the Americans are finally going to come and we're going to be a new state of the Union.

—Let it be the judge, repeated Don Baldomero.

He tapped his watch once more, finished his glass of brandy

---

*Alfonso Armada y Comyn was one of the top-ranking army officers (and secretary to King Juan Carlos) who plotted with Lieutenant-Colonel Antonio Tejero Molina of the Civil Guard to overthrow the Spanish government in the abortive coup of 23 February 1981.

and stood up by leaping from the heights of the stool like someone diving into a swimming pool.

Carlos looked into my eyes, put his hands on my shoulders, brought his face close to mine and said:

—As for me, I have no doubts, Lola.

He kissed me on the mouth and a gentle breeze stuck my clothes to my body as if I were naked.

His moving tongue made my mouth flood with saliva.

I felt dizzy.

We went to his house, the same studio in Calle San Marcos Carlos Clot the detective now occupied.

That night, for the only time in my life, I felt we weren't a man and a woman.

We were just what we are: inconsolable, irremediable creatures hanging on to one another.

In the morning the propellers of the Black Hawks woke us up. American troops were patrolling in jeeps and gifting cartons of Lucky Strike to the civil population. Six months later the Membership Treaty was voted through and the US Iberian Federation was founded. Life changed: a new life, a pencil with the lead broken inside.

Carlos was sincere. That night he'd wanted to sleep with me, without a doubt, but he was interested in nothing more than that. He didn't feel able to love anybody, not even Cati, who was his girlfriend. He only wanted to write *Profound Deafness* and disappear so as to become immortal. A path with no way forward and no way back.

So died my love, an innocent victim of Carlos's ambition, like I was later of Fernando's, perhaps.

Five years later, Carlos lay down on the floor with the manuscript of *Profound Deafness* and injected himself with an overdose.

He was wearing braces. He used them to clamp the manuscript against his chest.

He died on the same parquet Benito and I were treading on, he remained like a little bird, half on his side, with his legs rigid and his beak half open.

Clot examined the copies of the documents while sipping Loch Lomond.

One of them, in my father's handwriting, was a chemical formula. It was a copy of the original Estanis had handed over to Fernando.

The rest were the medical records of secret surgical operations carried out in the clinic.

CLOT POSITIONED THE PIECES on a chessboard and began playing an exhausting game against himself, because after every move he got up, went round the table and occupied the appropriate side of the board.

Why did I go to bed with Johnson that night?

If I hadn't done I wouldn't have been the innocent victim of a dastardly murder.

And why did Johnson leave me papers he knew might cost me my life? In order to wreak revenge on my father and on the clinic he was interned in? Why did he think they'd go after him whilst I'd run no risk, yet would know how to put those documents to good use?

The last night of my life, when we left Estanis's armour-plated villa, the four of us, Fernando, Mario, Eduardo and me, embarked on a municipal schooner and set a course for Malasaña. We tied up at San Ildefonso quay. On the esplanade they'd built a parking area that was full of bicycles. At this hour the city began to expand like the mercury in a thermometer and started prowling the load-bearing walls of apartment houses and shifting the streets, round plazas and memories of the pedestrians around.

We went to El Angie, El Morgenstern and El Penta, which had reopened and where they went on playing songs by Enrique Urquijo:

If I disappear I don't want
anyone to remember who I was.
Hold me tight, María,
hold me tight,
for this night's the coldest of all
and sleep eludes me.

Now I know that while we were listening to his voice in El Penta, on the other side of the square, on Espiritu Santo, Enrique Urquijo was already on the ground, head resting on his windcheater, his eyes open beneath the stars.

We entered El Acme, leaving the prints of our shoes in the sawdust on the floor. Mario had a hard-boiled egg with paprika and Eduardo took me to the toilet so I might see the countryside through the window: I recognised the sky of Alberchina, on a spring afternoon in 1975.

We ended up in El Pespunte.

All of a sudden I saw Johnson enter with his bag on his shoulder.

Fernando recognised him at once and got all rattled – now I know why. He and Estanis had undoubtedly been looking for him for ages.

Johnson found a space at the end of the bar and asked for a whisky and Sprite. I went to say hello.

When I looked behind me Fernando had disappeared. He must

have gone to warn Estanis, so that he in turn could warn the Boss and Brains.

Eduardo came over and I introduced them:

—Eduardo Sandoval, lyric poet. This is Johnson, an old friend.

They shook hands.

Later, on the third glass, I asked Johnson once again:

—Is it true you don't remember me? You met me many years ago, as soon as you arrived at the clinic. You called me Trompita, don't you remember?

—What are the dates, please?

—It must have been at the end of the seventies, Juanito Johnson, before the end of the oil and the Federation: before the life we lead.

—Zero. *Nada. Niente. Nihil obstat. Rien de rien.* That's impossible. I have no memories from before 1982. That was the date they operated on me. I forgot everything.

—What did they operate on you for, Johnson? asked Eduardo.

Johnson kept silent. He took a long swig of Sprite and then one of whisky. He looked right and left.

—I can't talk about that. It's super-top-secret.

—My lips are sealed, amigo, said Eduardo.

I think it was the combination of the childish phrase and the gesture of absolute seriousness with which he pronounced it that managed to gain Johnson's confidence; he ended up saying:

—A secret surgical operation.

—Where was this, Johnson? asked Eduardo.

—In Dr García Femater's clinic. In the black basement. They did a lobotomy on me.

—My father worked there at the time, Johnson. His name's Juan José Eguíbar, I confessed.

—I'm sorry for you, truly. But it's best that you know. There was secret brain surgery going on in the basement. They operated on me secretly. They were taking bits of their brain from the patients to produce tablets with. To plug the gap they put a parenthesis in my brain, whole years of my life between parentheses.

He explained how they'd extracted his past with an electric scalpel. He still remembered the whirring of the instrument. Then they kept him hidden for a time, until the traces of the intervention disappeared. Next, they let him out, with no memory of the last ten years and, according to what he told us, with a set of instructions implanted in his head through post-hypnotic suggestion.

With the passage of time he'd managed to reconstruct the odd memory and begun to suspect that he'd been operated on in the clinic's basement rooms. They turned him into a 'sleeper', he claimed. He had instructions installed in his brain and had no other recourse but to obey when he heard the keyword. He'd go on fulfilling orders without knowing it, when and as the predetermined keywords were activated by his hypnotisers.

—Just imagine. One day you fancy a meatball, but the decisive question's this: do you really fancy a meatball or are you only obeying without even knowing it? Maybe a word heard at the bar, the word *formwork*, for instance, has activated the next secret instruction: 'You desperately desire a meatball, eat a meatball right now.' Can you imagine it? My life's no life at all. I don't know if I do something because I want to or if I'm obeying the secret instructions implanted by the asylum orderlies.

Johnson told us he was afraid.

He wondered what terrible mission he was destined for. What

order would he have to carry out on hearing some seemingly innocent words like *formwork* or maybe *soda siphon*?

What could we tell him? That this was a paranoid delusion? That, sure, he'd been in the basement, in the Rest Unit, kept in isolation, but that nothing bad had happened there?

According to him, they were doing illegal but highly lucrative operations in that basement. Lobotomies, organ extractions for transplants and purloining neurones for the pharmaceutical and cosmetic industries.

That was where UgePharma came in, apparently, along with its main shareholder, Estanis Pérez Ugena.

—And my father, Johnson? I insisted.

—I remember nothing of your father, I assure you.

I understood that in fact he'd rebuilt his life, an interpretation that helped him understand what'd happened to him.

That's what delusion is: a version of the facts which, however nutty, turns out to be more acceptable than reality.

In the Rest Unit my father and García Femater had overdone it with the psycho-pharmaceuticals. It hit you in the eye. I myself had noticed something strange when he reappeared thirty pounds heavier and as if he functioned at half the RPM of before. In order to give meaning to that traumatic experience he'd come up with a delusion by which he explained adverse reality to himself.

The important thing isn't the delusion. What's terrible is to try and imagine what reality needs to cause such delusion in order to become tolerable.

He went staggering off to the toilet.

—He's the living symbol of the democratic transition and recent history, Eduardo observed. —No memories, no will of his own, unwittingly obeying secret orders from someone he doesn't know...

—We're all Johnsons, then, Eduardito.

—*Ich bin ein* Johnson.

—Yes, it's funny. I laughed reluctantly. In fact I suppose he's an example of what can happen with an over-strong chemical treatment.

—There are people who've stayed hooked on LSD. At any rate this is a magical encounter, Lola.

—Obviously, Eduardito: hocus-pocus.

Magic?

The life of the artiste was in danger.

At the end the girl cut in two will not reappear whole. My head, with its pretty face, and my body, with so many surplus pounds, remain separate, and the string of blood undone for all time.

As a result of magic, I suppose, Johnson and I stayed behind on our own and got lost in streets that were changing location and direction, like our lives. Hortaleza and Fuencarral ran north–south, Gran Vía was paved and the wind from Plaza de España brought the smell of the high seas and the murmur of waves.

Only the hidden motor of the mechanical ducks of Mariano de Cavia went on functioning with an implacable flapping of wings.

I told Johnson to come with me to my place, where he finally took off those shiny boxer shorts and at the end handed me some documents.

The rest is history: like me.

In the flat that was now Charlie Clot's in San Marcos Benito was studying the chessboard.

The detective was playing against himself, changing seat with every move and utilising one cerebral hemisphere to move the whites and the other the blacks.

On the board only the two kings and three pawns remained.

—I reckon this is a tie, I commented.

—I don't think so, Teach. They're in zugzwang, we've done it in school, it's a position in which the one whose turn it is to move loses.

—And whose move is it?

—No idea, Teach.

That's the way my life's been: zugzwang.

Then the doorbell rang.

It was Estanis, accompanied by the Boss and Brains. The Boss was wearing his prison gear, no belt or laces in his shoes; Brains had put his anorak in the anorak pocket itself and was wearing the lump strapped around his waist.

—Good evening, Mr Clot.

—Do we know each other?

—We have friends in common: Man Chopeitia, for example. I'm Pérez Ugena, of UgePharma, but you can call me Estanis. These two are nobodies, just telephone numbers in my diary. Neither do they hear, so we can talk freely.

—Have a seat, Mr Pérez Ugena, offered Clot.

—You're looking for certain papers, am I right? asked Estanis, sitting down on the sofa with care.

—You're wrong, I've already found them.

—And do you have copies of them?

—That's right.

—That's what I imagined. Surely you know they don't belong to you…

—Surely you know they've cost human lives.

—Yes, it's very sad, Mr Clot. Really very sad. But those papers will enable us to save lives, they're the basis for neuroprotein K666. Do you know what I'm talking about?

Clot nodded. He served himself a glass of Loch Lomond without offering Estanis one.

Maybe he'd divined he'd been a teetotaller since '81.

—Of course, Clot. Will you hand over the copies to me now? Estanis was moving his jaws as if he were crushing ice.

—Why should I do that?

—Come on, come on, don't be childish. Do you know what'll happen to your daughter if they stop giving her the treatment?

Clot closed his eyes to drink, pressing the whisky against his palate with his tongue, as if it were a painful and bitter memory.

—I know.

—Shall we swap picture cards, Clot? You give me those copies and your daughter will go on receiving the pills, what do you say?

Clot looked at the tips of his shoes and went over to the chessboard. With his index finger he pushed the white king, which rolled across the squares.

He took the papers from the inside pocket of his jacket and took a lighter to them.

—Good boy, Clot. I'll give Manex Chopeitia your regards.

On the point of burning his fingers, Clot flung the flaming documents on the floor, where they burned out.

Only ashes remained, growing cold in the same spot Carlos Viloria decided not to go on living or to annihilate the universe in.

When he closed the door behind Estanis, Charlie Clot contemplated the chessboard.

—There was no way forward and no way back: they were moving

the whites. Some life this is! he remarked to himself, adding, after a pause, —Because there ain't no other, otherwise…

The detective was drinking for a time and crying, without touching his face with his hands. Then he fell asleep on the sofa, gripping a bottle of Loch Lomond between his thighs without me being able to tell whether it was half full or half empty.

IT WAS A DIFFICULT SORT OF LOVE. I was dead, he was invented. He was fourteen, with an erection of less than four inches and fingernails bitten to the quick. I was about to reach the post-mortem age of thirty-six, I had the body I saw myself with inside my head and in that same bed, the night of the invasion, I'd slept for the only time with the love of my life, Carlos Viloria.

I unbuttoned the pharmacist's white coat and saw that the lad immediately began touching himself through the hole in his pocket.

—Take off your clothes, Beni, I whispered into his ear.

—Down to the underpants?

—The underpants too!

He removed his shoes and emptied them. He had enough sand inside to fill two hourglasses, his and mine.

He took off his jersey and vest in one go, just like his trousers and underpants. Then his socks. He was looking at me all engrossed and horny.

—The glasses too, love.

—Then I won't see a thing, Teach.

—Look at me with your hands, dumbo.

He pressed himself against me and remained immobile, his head turned the other way.

The lad knew no better. The only experiences I'd provided Benito with in my novels had all been below ground.

In the metro carriage he always travelled with a chest pressed against his back, a pubis that dovetailed with his hip, other men's dicks pushing against his abdomen, bits of bodies he was incapable of recognising. Like bursts of machine-gun fire he clocked his share of rounded breasts and thighs intuited in the turning of a skirt, handfuls of hairy, sweating flesh that he picked up hither and thither and stored away for his subsequent evocation and manual usage.

For Benito the metro had been much more than lewdness and often the exact opposite. He touched bodies, it's true, and saw ankles, legs, thighs, hands, necks and chests, but all as if they'd been painted by Francis Bacon, at once sublime and in a state of decomposition. You have to have travelled by metro in summer to become aware of the number of moles, wens, warts, birthmarks and sores most of us have. Down there, Benito encountered human flesh in all its unembraceable truth, at once attractive and repulsive, as steeped in time and death as in life and sexuality, lit by dim bulbs covered in a wire grille and visible only in bits, as if the passengers had just been cut to shreds, chopped up with a hatchet prior to entering the carriage.

The Cyclopean child got horny, it's true, but the metro was more serious and startling than a simple sexual experience. It must have been something of a metaphysical order, the same kind of education country kids get by sticking pins in birds' eyes.

—Come here, I whispered, pushing him towards the bed.

Charlie Clot was snoring on the sofa, the bottle balanced precariously.

His dream was drawing close to us, but in sleep nobody could see us either: I saw a headless woman and a blind man, Clot's father, who called him 'Carlitos, son'.

Benito lay on top of me and touched my breasts with his fingers. I took his dick in my right hand and slipped it inside me.

—I'm stuffing Teach, macho! I'm screwing 'er from Matracas!

Saying it out loud overexcited him. He came, psstt, like a splash of milk, all of a quick.

—That's it, Beni? That's all?

—Is something missing, Teach? What did I forget? He was going all red.

—Come here, lie on your back, close your eyes.

He tasted of sea salt and smelt of some cleaning product I didn't recognise, a window-cleaner, perhaps. His dick gradually grew in size between my lips, against my tongue, which was licking the gland in circles. I got up on top of him, put him inside me and began moving very slowly in a spiral, like a corkscrew, while I whispered:

—Do you like it? Look at me, look me in the eyes.

Benito's pupils were dilated and he wore an expression of panic. He felt pleasure and was afraid. He was biting his lips, clenching his fists and trembling like that leaf the wind's on the point of wresting from the tree.

In the meantime, the blind father fixed his eyes on us, without seeing us, and the headless woman probed the walls with her hands, seeking the rest of herself.

—You've a pretty face, Teach, Benito whispered.

For the first time in my life it didn't bother me. On the contrary: I felt happy.

I thought that attic on Calle San Marcos was going to come apart at the seams. The walls were sagging, the doors were creaking, they wanted to come off their hinges, the glass of water on the table shattered, wetting our foreheads, the feet of the furniture were splitting, the building's blocks of stone were giving way, the parquet was coming apart on its own and, blue, the stars were shimmering, not in the distance, though, but getting stuck in the vault of my palate, constellations of shooting stars that were bursting in my mouth like bubbles.

At that exact moment, the flowers in a vase suddenly opened.

I think they were roses, the petals formed a labyrinth.

We remained immobile, exhausted, emptied of our own selves.

It seemed as if the horizon had drawn back in order to surge forward to meet us.

I heard the din of breaking glass and twisted iron, like a head-on crash of two trains.

LIKE A THUNDERCLAP Clot's cough awoke us.

The detective put water on to boil in a cheap alloy saucepan and rinsed a cup he'd left for the night on the dresser with half an inch of liquid at the bottom so the coffee grounds wouldn't go hard.

Such dregs always make me think of death, the same as shoes side by side between the feet of a chair or the vision of empty clothing, without a person inside, hanging inside a dark wardrobe.

Dawn was breaking. On the pavement three pigeons were pecking at a puddle of reddish vomit, crepuscular in tone, like one of those dusks from *The Thousand Best Poems of All Time*. On the other side of the Castellana Canal Los Jerónimos was tying up. It manoeuvred with difficulty. Its towers were stained with saltpetre and it had a leak in the nave. The anchor was a bishop's tiara; the oars, crosiers; and the figurehead, a merciless Pantocrator sculpted in wood. An athletic canon leapt to the ground and from the deck they threw him a hawser. Once moored, they got down to caulking the church.

Clot drank his coffee with a dash of Loch Lomond. He took a

leak, didn't brush his teeth and went out on to the street in the same clothes he'd slept in on the sofa.

—Benito, what occurred last night will never happen again, I said to the boy. —We let ourselves get carried away. In that same apartment, years ago… In short, it's complicated. I don't regret anything, we did right, but it won't be repeated.

—Never again, Teach, I swear!

It surprised even me, but I believed him. He seemed sincere.

—We're going to see where Clot goes.

—Teach, it's just that I've gotta tell you something, he stammered.

—Later, Beni, we don't have time now.

—I've lied to you, Teach, he claimed.

—I've lied to you too, Benito. We'll talk about it in a while.

I told him to put the patch on his lazy eye and we left on the heels of the detective.

After a series of breakfasts, all of them of whisky drunk while leaning on different zinc-covered bars, Clot arrived at 9 a.m. at my parents' house.

My father was already dressed and the two of them sat in the kitchen, talking in whispers so as not to wake my mother.

—I'm sorry, Doc. There's no case. It was the madman, I've verified it, Clot said.

—Are you sure? I want proof.

—Your daughter slept with him, that much is proved. In the morning he must have blown his top and shot her. Elementary, my dear friend.

—And the gun? They haven't found the gun. I don't buy it,

Clot, I don't buy it. Johnson would never have blown his top in that way.

—He must have thrown the weapon into the Castellana Canal, you'll see how it turns up in the next drag they do. Clot looked my father in the eyes. —What's more, Johnson had a motive, as you well know, Dr Eguíbar.

My father was on the verge of tears.

—That isn't true, he said, between sobs. —I didn't operate on Johnson. It was Fernando. Dr Eguilaz, my son-in-law. And you know it, Clot, I left the clinic for that very reason.

Charlie Clot put a hand on my father's shoulder and spoke in a serene, almost indistinct voice:

—Of course I know, Doc, but did Johnson? That is the question. Maybe he thought you were responsible, right? Think about it.

My father was crying with his hands on his thighs and his eyes wide open. His chin trembled.

—Pull yourself together, Doc. You have to live. You have to forget: enough said, Clot recommended.

My father got to his feet and was standing at attention, almost.

—You're right, Charlie. I'm losing it, forgive me. To go on living you have to forget.

They hugged each other.

I started screaming, I told my father he was fooling him, that it wasn't true, that out of cowardice or to protect his daughter Clot had made a deal with my killers, that he was guilty of nothing.

My father couldn't hear me. I went on being inaudible, invisible, intangible: running water with no vessel to contain it, a life that doesn't fit into a single fulfilled desire.

I wanted to cry at my father's side, but the strand of blood between my heart and my head remained undone.

—You have to learn to forget, you've got to get control again, my father repeated.

Benito took me by the hand and led me to my old bedroom.

I lay down on my little bed.

WHAT WILL THEY REMEMBER of me? My laugh? My hands? My cough first thing in the morning? Some afternoon or other I've since forgotten? A wound on the knee they dressed when I was twelve?

Henceforth I'll only be what they go on recalling: a way of sitting, my velveteen skirt, my gesture of impatience when the phone rang. I'll exist only every now and then, when they suddenly remember me, like that banging against a piece of furniture in the corridor: unexpected, intense, much more painful than it seemed. At times they won't even be very sure what that thing they've bumped into in the dark might have been. I'll exist when least expected, summoned by a photo appearing in a drawer, a piece of paper between the pages of a book, or a landscape in which there's something of me, reddish vomit, vespertine in tone, like that clarity which still remains when the sun has already gone down and before it's completely dark.

There'll be recollections of me they'll go on banging against when they least expect it. Some will have a sharp corner: each time they get it on the shin they'll see stars.

The same thing's just happened to me.

One afternoon we were on the Alberchina reservoir and I was twelve years old. It was 1975. We were on the jetty. There were four canoes. There were four married couples (my parents, the Vilorias, the Solers and the Navalóns), plus Ignacio Eguilaz, Fernando's father.

It's taken me almost thirty years to realise they were flirting. It's hard to believe, but they were as young then as me now, not yet forty. The women were wearing bikinis, headscarves or turbans and those sixties sunglasses the size of a car windscreen and with outlandish frames. My mother had some turquoise-blue ones. The men wore red trunks and aviator-style Ray-Bans, with pear-shaped, greenish lenses. I imagine that if someone was carrying what at the time was known as a 'fagbag' it'd be Ignacio Eguilaz, the widower surgeon.

I don't know who had the idea. As if the prize were the women's admiration, the four men decided to have a race to the rock.

In the shed there were only three oars.

—We're a paddle short, Ignacio Eguilaz pointed out.

He was that kind of person, he didn't say skis but boards; never sticks, but rods; he did what he called 'footing'* and at times wore two-tone shoes. Maybe a 'fagbag', too, I don't recall, but he'd have been quite capable of it. Now Ignacio Eguilaz, the surgeon, is in a home, he no longer remembers who he is nor does he recognise his son. He has Alzheimer's. Maybe one day his son's neuroprotein K666 will restore his memory to him.

My father offered to go to the office to get another oar.

It'd be a mile there and a mile back, and I looked upon him at

---

*The Spanish word for 'jogging'.

the time as a hero. My father was capable of anything and thanks to him everything was possible: he didn't walk, he started running and wouldn't even take thirty minutes.

In those thirty minutes, while my father was sweating beneath the late-afternoon sun; while he asked Aquilino, the warden, for another oar; while he came back trotting along the gravel path, with the sun in his eyes, changing the oar from hand to hand, wiping the sweat from his brow with his arm; in the thirty minutes during which my father was a hero something happened that made him cease to be one: the Pérez Ugenas appeared, Paco and his son Estanis.

The two came recently showered and in shorts. Estanis had an oar in his hand.

The Pérez Ugenas had been unable to think of anything better than taking it to their house to paint. It was already dry and glistened, as if they'd varnished it.

—Waterproofing enamel, Paco Pérez Ugena explained.

—Maybe it'll give even more force to the stroke, commented Ignacio Eguilaz.

They were two of a kind, the fathers of Estanis and Fernando.

Francisco Pérez Ugena, who always had to be called Paco, was a record producer, so he lived in another world, one more brilliant and attractive than ours, because at the time my father was a resident in psychiatry, he'd just got to Madrid and the mechanical ducks of Mariano de Cavia, we had a blue 1430, and each time we left a light on when exiting a room he told us he didn't work for the electricity company. The life of the Pérez Ugenas, on the other hand, was like that oar: recently painted, waterproof, it even seemed varnished. Paco Pérez Ugena knew the famous, he spoke of Milan the way someone says Valdeacederas and drank dry martinis as if they were pop. Estanis once gave Fernando a photo of Kiko Ledgard dedicated by Kiko himself and Fernando brought it to school.

Women adored Paco Pérez Ugena. I wonder whether my mother did too. I reckon so.

Years later, Estanis's father went bankrupt and his son had to start from scratch, with shady property deals and a notebook with the phone numbers of individuals who carried firearms.

I remember it well, it was Ignacio Eguilaz, the widower-surgeon, Fernando's father, who first said there were now enough paddles to begin the race.

My heart skipped a beat and fluttered, as if it were passing without shock absorbers over those rows of sleeping policemen at the entrance to the housing estate.

I thought of my father, who went on running, all sweaty, while the recently showered Paco Pérez Ugena grinned.

He was never in the right place at the right time, the poor sod, he always wore the least appropriate clothes, it was his destiny.

Navalón and Soler were the only ones who suggested waiting for him.

—Juan can't be long, they said.

—While he's in the process of arriving, we can have a race, suggested Pérez Ugena, Estanis's father.

The four of them got into their canoes, with the recently showered Pérez Ugena in the place my father was to have occupied.

Mercedes Navalón gave the starting signal by waving a handkerchief in the air.

Pérez Ugena was in front from the very first. He rowed like a professional. He paddled in the direction of the horizon and I looked the other way, in the direction of the office, waiting to see my father arrive running.

I heard the applause of the women at the same time as I saw the silhouette of my father, who was raising the oar above his head in a gesture of victory.

He arrived exhausted and smiling. I hugged him.

—The Pérez Ugenas have brought the missing oar, they'd taken it to paint.

My father didn't ask any questions.

Prior to speaking, I momentarily glimpsed a look in his eyes I didn't understand. His pupils seemed like crystal, but a crystal from another planet, like a lunar stone with mysterious properties, a piece of glass that could burn with a flame without splitting or get red hot without shattering – that was the impression he gave me.

I must have looked worried, because he said:

—It's all right, Lola, lass, it's all right. You have to live. To live for real, you have to know how to lose. That's the secret, all the rest is unimportant. It's all right, and he went back to looking at me like always with his bluish-green eyes, the colour of a gentle kind of water I'd never lose my footing in.

In point of fact I didn't feel worried, for my father transmitted the conviction that in life, this life, it's always better to have gone for the oar than to have participated in the race.

They returned rowing slowly, joking. My father applauded. They heaved the canoes on to the jetty and left the oars in the shed.

—Juanjo, macho, give us a hug! demanded Paco Pérez Ugena.

It was the only time I head someone call my father Juanjo, his friends always called him Juan or Juan José, and only Uncle Frankie dared call him Jota.

That was the one thing that really produced an anxious, incomprehensible feeling in me: I was ashamed, I felt I shouldn't have heard it, shouldn't have heard someone calling my father Juanjo, as if I'd seen something forbidden or had come upon them naked on opening the door without knocking.

I felt guilty without knowing why. I'm beyond hope.

My father, with the oar in his hand, let himself be hugged by Pérez Ugena.

I started crying.

My father came up to me and put his hands on my shoulders. In my ear he repeated that it was all right.

Then we heard the click of the camera. It was Ignacio Eguilaz, Fernando's father, who'd just taken a photo.

I first saw it long afterwards, when they finally took the film to be developed months later. It was in black and white: I came out at the side of my father, I was crying and I was wearing a tartan kilt.

While the women were congratulating the winner, without saying anything my father went over to the shed. He opened the door very slowly, put the oar he'd brought next to the others, and carefully closed it. He's always been very precise in his movements. Afterwards he joined the group, smiling.

I'd already stopped crying.

There wasn't another race, it was almost night-time and, furthermore, I remember what I thought: now there's a canoe less because there's a father more.

We went to the club for a drink and nobody mentioned the business of the oars or my father's run to the office.

In the club were the lads, the sons of Viloria and of Ignacio

Eguilaz, Carlos and Fernando; and also the Navalóns' little boy, Mario, and Vicente Soler.

My father forgot that afternoon, he told me when I reminded him of it years later, but I've never forgotten that look in his eyes prior to him telling me it was all right.

Since then all I've had to do is think of his eyes in order not to feel alone, whatever happens.

To be at his side, even now, even here, all I have to do is clasp in my fist that bit of lunar rock, that pebble from an unknown outer space.

On the other hand, if I think of that diminutive, Juanjo, I instantly go red, as if I were remembering a shameful act, something that was my fault and which I regretted but which I could do nothing about, anyway.

I don't know whether I've understood my father's life, but I do know that, for me, it all fits into that look in his eyes, that precious stone proceeding from the sidereal dark, into the eyes he looked at me with when he told me it was all right, that in order to live you have to know how to lose.

And my own? Have I managed to understand my life?

I suppose not, even seen from this other side. I don't understand it but I do know that all I don't understand of my life, its invisible centre, fits entirely into the feeling of shame I got from hearing my father called Juanjo, and in that question: why do I feel guilty? What of?

Mother, I hear you walking. You're alone, Mum. I hear you, you're walking through my heart in the dark. Be careful, don't bang into the feet of the furniture, into the sharp edge of the life I've led. Mum, you're walking towards the end of the corridor, touching the walls lightly with your hands, but where's the light switch? How can I help you?

TEACH! TEACH! WAKE UP! Miss Silvia! Benito Viruta was shaking me vigorously.

—What's up, Beni?

—Here's the light switch, Miss Silvia, it's all right.

I must have talked in my sleep because the kid had turned on the light.

It seemed to me Benito was worried and, maybe for the first time in his life, dependent on someone other than himself.

My parents were watching the telly.

—Teach, you don't want to go on this way, right? The way we are now.

It surprised me that Benito should say it.

Actually, what were we doing there, posthumous, incorporeal, a pair of gawpers, that boy and me, gazing on other people's dreams, without being able to touch anything or be reflected in mirrors, seeing loved ones suffer and being unable to console them or weep with them?

Of course I didn't want to go on that way, the way we were now. The young shaver was right.

I was terrific, it's true, with a stunning body and without

dioptres, but the fact of the matter is I missed my own body, the one that was below the sodden earth of La Almudena, I wanted each one of my hundred and thirty-two pounds, all my spare tyres, the rubbing of one thigh against the other when walking. I was very tired of waiting for my fluttering, flyaway Dasein in vain.

I've always wanted to live.

The trouble is I don't fit into one single desire. I wanted to live, but I also wanted not to die, ever.

What was happening to me, that only one of my desires would be fulfilled, was a nightmare: I went on living, sure, but after being dead. Or the opposite, I dunno: I wasn't completely dead, but I was no longer alive.

I wanted to live, to live a human life, although that would include death, annihilation, nothingness: the ultimate desire concealed beneath all those desires I didn't fit into.

I wasn't prepared to survive that way, to remain that way, to prolong myself that way, as I would never have been prepared to survive like Fernando, via a Nobel Prize, or like Carlos, via a masterpiece of literature.

In order to go on that way I preferred to be dead. To really live you have to learn to die.

It was what my father said.

I needed my tiny life, unfinished, with my own meaningless death.

—Of course not, Beni, I then replied to the kid.

—I've lied to you, Teach, confessed the boy. —This won't end until you finish the novel, my novel.

—But I can't write, Benito!

—I can. From his trouser pocket he took a clapped-out pen and a notebook. —All you have to do is dictate it to me. That's what I hadn't told you.

—You've always known it?

—Yes, Teach. Forgive me. I wanted to be at your side.

I remained indecisive, almost stunned, looking at the trembling, sincere and shamefaced boy.

—And what'll happen to you, Benito?

—What has to happen, don't you worry about me, Teach, really.

—I've also lied to you, Benito. I'm not Miss Silvia, I revealed to him.

—You're not 'er from Matracas, Teach? So who is, then?

—Benito, I'm your mother. It's me: Mum.

—Mum? His voice trembled.

—I'm Mum.

He began crying.

—Mum, look at me.

I hugged him and looked him in the eyes.

—I want you to write me. Write me, Mum. I want you to. Make a clean copy of me.

He opened the notebook and took the ink-stained pen.

I started dictating. The kid wrote with effort, sticking the tip of his tongue out and pressing hard as he wrote in a clear hand.

I changed the ending. Benito went out into the street, he abandoned that basement and managed to see the other people from head to toe and not just their footfalls making off indifferently or getting threateningly closer.

Of *The Thousand Best Poems of All Time*, I took the only one I found in the pocket of a dead poet to tack together the tear in the kid's trouser pocket.

I dictated the final sentences: '...and then, without the fact that she was the ugliest girl in the class or the finger she was missing on her left hand bothering him, Benito Viruta brought his lips to Esther Martínez's. That way he made much more sense, much more than he had before. They kissed with their eyes closed in order to see the blue days and the sun of childhood.'

—That's it, Teach?

—It's ready. Take your patch off, you don't need it now.

I hugged him.

I remembered Nietzsche, the day he went mad and embraced the beaten horse to protect it from the coachman's whip.

I was also ending up interposing myself between the maltreated Benito and whoever was mercilessly punishing him.

It was I who was wielding the whip.

And Benito was also me: the child of my imagination.

I was protecting myself from myself, just as in school, in those Houses of Torture or in Viloria versus Viloria.

—Thanks, Mum. I love you. I love you a lot, said Benito between the tears.

—I love you too.

A butterfly approached, beating its wings, and alighted on the kid's tousled hair.

—*Adiós*. And jaaackpooooot! Keep the change! exclaimed the boy.

—That's it, Beni, you've learned. Let life keep its own change. Jackpot!

I remained hugging his neck with my eyes closed.

When I opened them again Benito had disappeared.

Then I saw another butterfly, my Dasein, my rainy heart, my fluttering, telltale heart, which was flying over my head.

The string of blood knotted itself and at last I was able to weep floods.

—Now you've really done it! my psyche accused me.

With open wings it settled on my forehead. The curtains open. Out comes a woman with a pretty face, she meets a man, isn't happy and next they kill her. The curtains close.

What's the name of the movie?

Fiction
Crime
Noir

Culture
Music
Erotica

dare to read at serpentstail.com

Visit serpentstail.com today to browse and buy our books, and to sign up for exclusive news and previews of our books, interviews with our authors and forthcoming events.

| NEWS | cut to the literary chase with all the latest news about our books and authors |

| EVENTS | advance information on forthcoming events, author readings, exhibitions and book festivals |

| EXTRACTS | read the best of the outlaw voices – first chapters, short stories, bite-sized extracts |

| EXCLUSIVES | pre-publication offers, signed copies, discounted books, competitions |

| BROWSE AND BUY | browse our full catalogue, fill up a basket and proceed to our fully secure checkout – our website is your oyster |

FREE POSTAGE & PACKING ON ALL ORDERS...
ANYWHERE!

sign up today – join our club